Blood on the Breakwater

Jean Paetkau

Contact
e: jeanworks@yahoo.ca
t: Snufflewort
i: Snufflewort_
f: facebook.com/Snufflewort

Kids books by Jean Paetkau:

Rumpa and the Snufflewort
The Bumwuzzle Rescue
The Snufflewort Haunting

Dedication

This story is dedicated to the marvellously
quirky, eccentric and artistic residents of James Bay
who make this neighbourhood a community.

And also to my tweeter peeps.
Thank you for sharing sunsets and stories.

And to
Jason
Laura
Andrea
Haley
&Jacob.

Chapter 1

The sun began its leisurely descent toward the ocean's horizon, infusing the clouds with pinks and purples, heralding the end of day. Along the exposed side of the historic cement and granite breakwater in the Victoria harbour, waves splashed gently and then receded. It was an unseasonably warm and tranquil evening in early March, and the slender walkway stretched across the azure waters like the arched arm of an elegant ballerina, above which seagulls danced on the currents of a mellow yet lyrical wind.

Having left her wool cap at home, Helene was grateful for a balmy breeze — her daily walk was always more restorative when the weather welcomed her like a friend. She took heavy rains and blasting winds as a personal affront.

Walking the length of the breakwater a few blocks from home was her daily ritual. The routine was an attempt to keep the stress and grinding exhaustion of parenting and work at bay. As a single mother, she had neither the freedom nor the finances for international vacations bookended by long plane trips, so her excursions were acutely local.

The thirty-minute journey was reassuringly familiar, but it also held enough variation to be refreshing. It was impossible to stray from the path: railings on both sides kept one safe from explorations that might lead to a frigid plunge in the Pacific. But the shifting sky reflected an infinite spectrum of moods, a vivid canvas of a mutable painting.

The concrete and granite breakwater had been completed in 1917 to lure trade by way of the newly constructed Panama Canal. It was built to protect ships

1

unloading at the piers from winds and waves blowing through the strait between Victoria and the Washington coastline. Like many places in Canada, it was named after a fur trader, honouring the legacy of Peter Ogden while predictably ignoring the history of the local Lekwungen-speaking Peoples. The area had recently been rebranded from Ogden Point to the Breakwater District. And in 2013, the safety railings were added to the walkway, a reassuring change Helene appreciated when her gaze was affixed to the sky.

Just as previous generations had wound up grandfather clocks to keep the rhythm of their days, Helene needed to return to the breakwater each evening. But instead of turning the gears tighter, the daily pilgrimage released the tension that had built up since waking that morning. It gave her the patience and energy to deal with another day of packing school lunches before sunrise and unpacking government press releases until sunset.

Helene had been a journalist for more than a dozen years. She was drawn to the profession by the thrill and responsibility of telling stories that had the power to create change, especially in the lives of the most disenfranchised. But before going into broadcasting, she had spent the beginning of her thirties teaching history to teenagers, a different kind of storytelling that involved chalkboards and attendance sheets instead of a radio and microphone. Ultimately, it was the desire to create new stories rather than retelling old ones, from questionable textbooks, that made her pursue a career in broadcasting.

In the years before she had become a teacher, she had dabbled in many other jobs, including everything from glass blowing to renting out shoes in a bowling alley. Maybe that was one of the things she loved most about her walk on the breakwater: there was only one path to choose from, with a lighthouse and wooden wind-ravaged benches at the farthest point. Sometimes no options could be the best option.

The Victoria harbour was busy with activity that evening, on the water and in the air. A whale-watching boat was returning from a trip that promised a close encounter with the orcas that fed in the waters off the coast. There was a thrum of helicopter blades as travellers with more money than time began a journey to Vancouver. A quieter seaplane also skated across the sky, possibly on its way to one of the more remote Gulf Islands. In the distance, several massive freighters were anchored while awaiting an open dock to unload their goods, and a solo kayaker splashed their paddle in the waters close to shore.

Like most evenings, the people walking along the breakwater were a mix of strangers and familiar faces. An oversized tour bus had disgorged a group of boisterous Americans in garish running shoes and pastel golf shirts. Although their noisy presence was an irritation, Helene envied the fact that they were taking in the spectacular scenery for the first time, eagerly snapping selfies with Washington's Olympic mountain range as the backdrop. Local residents who walked the breakwater lacked the enthusiasm displayed by the tourists, but they possessed the unmistakable serenity of those whose homes had a vista of the ocean.

Helene was a transplant herself, having grown up in a prairie province known for oil and beef and men who thought trucks were more powerful than the poems of a Czech dissident. The vast blue Alberta sky had been a stand-in ocean, offering the promise of escape from the sensation of being a foreigner in her land-locked town. Having now raised her own children on the beaches of the West Coast, with endless afternoons spent collecting sea glass like shards of a shattered rainbow, she could not imagine living away from the water. To lose proximity to the ocean would be like giving up a second sky — a sky that also held a kind of oxygen essential to breathing.

The sun was just about to slip behind the horizon when Helene reached the bend in the breakwater path, a little more than halfway to the lighthouse at the end. Out of the corner of her eye, she spotted a misshapen object floating in the water, demanding her attention like an incongruous detail in a newspaper photograph.

Trying to make sense of the anomaly, her mind did a word association, except with images. Shifting from the familiar to the almost unfathomable.

Driftwood.

Seaweed.

Driftwood and Seaweed.

An animal.

An otter.

Or even a seal.

Too big.

Too much blood.

Too human.

A green and yellow checked scarf wrapped around a neck, trailing in the water like a flag of death.

Even as her mind tried to deny what her eyes already believed, her instincts as a journalist took over. If there was one thing people who spent their days in newsrooms were good at, it was emergencies. Disasters were like defibrillators for reporters — they made them come to life. Feel important. Full of purpose. It was everyday existence that they were bad at, hence the reputation for stocking booze as an office supply.

Helene followed the standard steps of an emergency response like an automaton. Knowing it was best to get support from another bystander, she turned to a tall man with a long gait who was heading in her direction.

"Do you have a phone?" the journalist asked the stranger. "Call 911!"

4

As the stunned man obediently retrieved his phone from an inside pocket, Helene did her best to offer an explanation. "There's someone down there, on the edge of the breakwater. A woman, I think. I'm going to try to reach her. You stay here. Ask for an ambulance. But also the police." From the way the waves were washing over the body, like a gentle undertaker, Helene believed the woman was beyond the aid of paramedics. But even spending more than a dozen years in a newsroom hadn't completely hardened her heart to hope.

Helene had to race forward another twenty feet along the breakwater before coming to one of the three stairways leading to the lower level. She swung open the small gate and tramped noisily down the metal stairs with ridges in the planks to prevent people from slipping when they were wet.

Once she reached the bottom of the stairs, she turned back in the direction from where she had come. It was trickier walking on the sea-level path because it was made up of giant blocks of granite, each three feet wide. Sometimes there was a gap between the massive cubes, so she had to take small leaps with the ocean waves lapping below. Concentrating on not losing her footing was a good way to distract her mind from the inert body that was her destination.

But only too soon Helene found herself standing on the rocky edge of a granite block, looking down at the figure in the water. It was a young woman whose dark hair was drifting lazily like the tentacles of a jellyfish, a few strands splayed across her closed eyes and open mouth in a way that made Helene yearn to brush them back in a motherly gesture.

Most of the coverage of disasters and deaths Helene had done as a journalist were from the hive of a chaotic newsroom. Phones ringing relentlessly. Multiple TV monitors blaring. But standing on the breakwater, looking down at the wasted, thin body, Helene had never felt so alone. She desperately wished for the presence of another human whose heart was still in working order.

Helene's attention was drawn to the sound of a horn in the distance, and she glanced up to see a yellow Coast Guard boat coming round the corner of the breakwater lighthouse. The journalist suspected the vessel was too late to rescue the young woman from death, but at least it was in time to save Helene from keeping vigil with a corpse.

As the emergency vessel made its rapid approach, Helene simultaneously felt relief and fresh anxiety. She would gladly give up the mantle of watching over the dead to someone in a position of authority. However, most police officers treated journalists with only slightly less contempt and suspicion than a convicted felon — especially journalists who happened to stumble on a crime scene.

As the boat pulled up alongside the breakwater, its loud engines falling silent, Helene took one last opportunity to look directly at the body in the ocean. The dark hair, the bloated skin, the ragged pale lips, a face forever altered by a mask of death.

Trying to steady her thoughts, Helene took a deep breath and then slowly exhaled. At the same time, she noticed that the wind had become stronger, almost aggressive, like it had sensed a disturbance in the equanimity of the evening.

Crashing against a breakwater boulder, the spray of a salty wave whipped against Helene's cheek, as though the ocean was offering tears she had yet to shed.

Chapter 2

The sky had grown a shade darker when Helene finally found herself sitting in the small cabin of the Coast Guard boat, watching tea slosh back and forth in the grey pottery mug she was holding. The journalist thought the movement of the liquid was an accurate reflection of what was going on in her stomach. But she didn't know if her inner agitation was caused by the relentless rocking of the vessel or the haunting face of the dead woman. Probably a bit of both.

"Take small sips," urged the Coast Guard officer who was standing at the helm. "It will help with the shock."

Helene wanted to protest that she was a seasoned journalist and was unfazed by the unfolding events, but another wave of nausea kept her from speaking. Trying to avoid splashing the hot drink on her hands, she lifted the mug to her lips and took a gulp.

Although admittedly disturbed by the discovery of a dead body on her evening outing, Helene was also unsettled by the fact that she was on a boat. For as much as she wanted to live near the water, she had always avoided being on the water. Helene feared boats the way others did airplanes, morbidly aware of the endless depths and darkness below. It was simply a matter of trust, or lack thereof, that the vessel would keep its promise to stay afloat.

Feeling suddenly self-conscious, Helene looked up to meet the gaze of the officer who was studying her with open concern. He was a younger man, who, despite the present circumstances, seemed to exude an enthusiasm for life. Blond hair escaped from the sides of a baseball cap, and although his face was bronzed it was not yet lined by the sun. Wearing a bright life vest and practical utility pants, he looked like he had never experienced the draining illumination of office fluorescent lights. Helene acknowledged a moment of passing jealousy for his undiminished vitality, especially when contrasted in her mind with the lifeless body she had stumbled on.

"I'm sorry we can't leave right away. I have to wait until more officers arrive, to keep the area secure."

Despite wanting to be anywhere else in the world at that moment, Helene nodded in understanding.

"I'm Jeff, by the way. Jeff Anders."

"Helene Unger," she responded, leaving out *nice to meet you*, as there was nothing nice about the situation.

When the Coast Guard officer had first arrived at the breakwater, he helped Helene step unsteadily onto the boat. Then he returned to the pathway and lifted the dead woman's body out of the water and laid it onto the granite blocks. Helene only watched his movements out of the corner of her eye — she knew there were some things you could never unsee.

"Do you think she drowned?" Helene found herself blurting out the question while still tightly holding onto the cup of tea. She was trying to bring some order to the situation by asking questions.

"Not unless the ocean has learned how to fire a gun," Jeff answered. "And probably close-up, considering the size of the hole in her chest."

Helene was alarmed — she had presumed the wounds on the body had come from crashing into rocks.

"Of course, she still could have drowned, depending on how long it took her to die," Jeff added in a quieter voice.

Helene felt a mixture of excitement and dread. A murder was a story that demanded unravelling, the lifeblood of her profession. But it also meant she was a witness to a crime. And that made everything more complicated. Would she even be allowed to cover this story, considering she had

8

discovered the body? She was already crafting arguments to persuade her radio producer.

Her racing thoughts were interrupted by the arrival of half a dozen uniformed police officers on the breakwater above. One of their number unfurled yellow tape across the path, to preserve the scene and keep gawkers at bay. When two others started to unroll a body bag, Helene looked away again.

As the uniformed officers secured the area, a slender woman in an olive-green vest and tall black rubber boots made her way onto the boat. The grimace on her face as she entered the cabin made Helene wonder if she also had no enthusiasm for watercrafts. Possessing a beauty that was incongruous to the horrors of the situation, the female officer looked like a model from the 1970s. She had high cheekbones, hazel eyes and sleek brown hair unruffled by death or humidity. Helene wondered if her looks were an asset or a hindrance when dealing with the criminal element.

The female officer surveyed the mariner and the journalist before introducing herself.

"Detective Kalinowski," she stated without extending a hand to shake. She then focused her attention on Helene. "I assume you're the one who found the body."

Helene nodded and then nervously launched into a description of how her regular evening walk had ended in a very irregular way. She shared how the air was warm and the sunset was brilliant, but the detective seemed unimpressed by these scene-setting details.

"Did you see anyone behaving in an unusual manner during your walk?" asked the police officer, after Helene had finished her outline of the events, ending with her boarding the Coast Guard boat.

"Nothing that stands out," responded Helene after a moment of consideration. "Just the usual mix of tourists and locals."

"Well, here's my card, in case you remember anything. You can reach me by email and cell." Detective Kalinowski passed Helene a small piece of stiff paper she had retrieved from one of the many pockets of her green vest. "And I also need to get your details. Name, number, where you live and work."

Helene had been bracing for the moment she disclosed that she was a journalist, and it went about as badly as she expected.

"A journalist? Christ," muttered the detective. "You know you can't publish any details from the scene until we've shared it with the public."

"I know my job," Helene responded defensively. "This isn't my first murder."

Detective Kalinowski raised her eyebrows. "Who said anything about murder?"

"Just a guess," Helene backpedalled. "She wasn't dressed for a swim."

"It's those kinds of details that you must keep to yourself. If you remember something significant, it needs to end up in an email to me, not on the front page of a newspaper. I'll call you tomorrow morning so you can come by the station and sign your statement."

Helene was tempted to point out to the detective that social media posts, not newspaper headlines, were how information was spread these days. But she didn't want to say anything to prolong the encounter.

"Do you mind helping us move the body? It's going to be an hour's wait for the paramedics to show up. There's still a serious staffing shortage." Detective Kalinowski was now speaking to the Coast Guard officer.

After Kalinowski and Jeff stepped off the boat, Helene assumed she was alone, not a state she found particularly comforting after such a close encounter with death. However, she was soon joined by another Coast Guard officer who walked into the cabin. Helene observed that this man was middle-aged, with a broad chest, muscular rather than thin. She imagined he might be a sort of mentor to Jeff.

The man smiled gently as if to put Helene at ease, but the warmth did not reach his eyes, which possessed an undeniable sadness. Dark greying hair peeked out from under a woollen cap knit in the geometric Coast Salish style.

"It's terrible what a man can do to another man. Or a woman. Then use the ocean as a graveyard."

Helene winced in response to his statement. He was obviously one of those people who could sum up a situation in a way that needed no further comment — the type to give journalists short interviews with great quotes.

"I'm Lee, by the way," the man continued, "and you should get back to your home. The light will be gone from the sky soon. It's not good to be in the dark after death has paid a visit."

"Helene," she introduced herself to this man who seemed to choose each word with great care. "Yes, home sounds nice. My children are probably wondering where I am." The journalist had an immediate and fierce longing to be cuddled up with her kids in bed. She knew their warm bodies would vanquish the chill in her hands and heart.

Lee peered out the window intensely, as if examining the horizon for threats, "That's good. To have children. I'll make sure Jeff gets you back to them quickly."

With that short exchange, the older mariner stepped out of the cabin. But Helene had less than a minute to reflect on the slightly odd encounter before the younger officer returned.

"Do you want me to take you straight into the harbour? It's getting a bit dark for walking on the breakwater." Obviously, Lee had kept his word and urged his colleague to return her to the shore. And as much as she yearned to get off the boat, she also didn't have the energy to complete her breakwater trek on foot, especially as there was only a sliver of moon to guide her. She looked up at the officer and

11

stated, "Take me to the beach, please. My house is just a couple blocks away."

Turning to face the helm, Jeff revved the engine and did a wide U-turn in the water. Helene had a fleeting thought as to whether his older colleague was on the vessel or if he was standing guard over the crime scene, like a sentinel above the frothing waves. Lee had the kind of presence that might bring a sort of comfort, even to the dead.

As they headed back to shore, waves crashing against the sides of the boat, the view of the breakwater's silhouette from the cabin window was a new and not entirely welcome perspective. The stone walkway seemed stripped of the solace and strength it had previously possessed. The journalist experienced a surge of grief, for the woman who lost her life but also for the breakwater that had been stripped of its allure — soiled forever, even after the waves had washed the blood away.

Chapter 3

"You got the 11:30?"

"Yes, I've got the 11:30."

"With the ferry delays?"

"Absolutely, but I'll check for the latest before I go to air."

After spending more than a decade in a newsroom, Helene no longer felt nervous about being on the radio. In fact, she preferred broadcasting the news to 50,000 listeners to attending a dinner party with half a dozen individuals she barely knew as some sort of pretense of maintaining a social life. She did her best to bypass casual interactions, as her idea of small talk was the latest update on the war in Ukraine. And at all costs she avoided schoolyard conversations with other mothers, involving discussions about kitchen renovations and spring break holidays, neither of which Helene could afford.

When she had arrived at the office the morning after discovering the body, her producer Riya Patel had asked her to prepare and deliver the 11:30 newscast. Normally this was the responsibility of the early reporter, but they were out sick that day. Helene had agreed to the request without protest as staff in a newsroom were like a crew at sea, simply taking over the jobs that needed doing. Keeping the newsroom moving through the currents of evolving and breaking stories was all that mattered.

Without looking at a clock, Helene knew she had twenty minutes before heading into the radio booth to turn on the mic and read the news. Like other radio journalists, she had developed an internal watch that precisely gauged the passage of time. She could measure minutes and seconds the way a chef added spices and flour without the need of teaspoons or scales. Or maybe it was more like a blacksmith who knew the moment a piece of iron was hot enough to hammer into shape on the anvil. The passage of time was a crescendo that built to the moment a newscast started or a broadcast concluded. Helene sometimes wondered if you held a stethoscope to the chest of a radio journalist whether you would hear the ticking of a second hand instead of a beating heart.

Picking up the phone on her desk, Helene was confident she had time for a short conversation before printing off her news script.

"Detective Kalinowski," answered the voice at the other end of the line, omitting any conversational pleasantries.

"Hello, Detective, it's Helene Unger again." The journalist had stopped by the station early in the morning to sign her witness statement for the officer. She had wanted to avoid being late for work and having to offer an explanation.

"Is there something else you needed to add to your statement?" The detective's curiosity was piqued.

Deciding a direct approach was best, Helene asked bluntly, "I was wondering if you had identified the victim yet."

"I'm impressed with your faith in my investigation, but we've only just gotten started. And anyway, that kind of information will be released to the public when we're ready. I hope you aren't asking for some kind of special treatment?" asked the officer.

"Not special treatment," said Helene while leaning back and tapping a pencil on the arm of her chair, "although I do feel like I have a vested interest in helping figure out what happened to that woman."

For a moment the line went quiet as Detective Kalinowski considered how to respond. Helene resisted the urge to break the silence herself.

"This is off the record," Kalinowski finally continued, with some hesitation, "but the fact is, we aren't getting anywhere very quickly. The victim had no ID on her, and sharing a picture of a corpse isn't the best idea. We're working up an artist sketch, but those are always a bit of a long shot."

"And no one has reported her missing yet?"

"She doesn't match any existing profiles."

"Okay, well, I do appreciate you sharing how things are going so far, even if it's not far at all," stated Helene before offering a quick goodbye and hanging up. The clock in her head was ticking a little more loudly, letting her know it was time to print off the script for the newscast and check for any last-minute ferry delays between the islands and the mainland. But another idea, which had been sparked by the phone call, was also forming in the back of her mind.

A few minutes later, Helene came out of the radio studio, threw her paper script into the recycling bin and clicked on the window of her favourite social media site, which was already open on her computer monitor. She had an idea of how to push forward the murder investigation, realizing her compulsion to share photos on social media had created a trove of visual data.

The journalist went for a walk on the breakwater practically every day, and she took photographs on most of these excursions. The long, clean lines of the pathway, and how they converged through the magic of perspective, were an irresistible draw to the human eye. Add to that the backdrop of a molten sunset, and even the amateur photographer came back with something worthy of a social media post. Over the months and years of walking on the breakwater, Helene had challenged herself to find a unique way of photographing the path on every visit, so she now had literally hundreds, if not thousands, of photos, most of which had been uploaded to her online profile.

15

As a rule, Helene avoided photographing people as she found they polluted the geometric cubism of the breakwater set against the impressionist sky. However, the more beautiful the sunset, the busier the breakwater became, so sometimes she had no choice but to include figures or risk missing the shot. This meant she had a personal archive of visitors to the ocean pathway, many of whom were locals on a daily pilgrimage to the lighthouse.

Sifting through her photographs with the speed of a journalist trained in the art of skimming massive reports for salient details, Helene wasn't entirely sure she would recognize the dead woman. When she had first come across the corpse, the facial features had been distorted by bloating and bruises. However, Helene recalled the woman's green and yellow checked scarf, short coat, and long, dark hair. She also thought that she might be able to intuitively spot the image of the woman whose body she had discovered.

Scanning the blurred faces and clothing in the background of her photographs, hoping for some flicker of recognition, Helene felt the familiar frustration of knowing that she would never learn the stories of the countless people she passed each day. Their births, their deaths, their abandoned aspirations would remain a mystery, like foreign countries she would never visit. But she knew a journalist had limited time to tell a certain number of stories. So she had to prioritize. And right now, the dead woman was at the top of her list.

Taking a moment to rest her brain from the rapid viewing of images, Helene paused to closely examine a shot of a heron perched on a floating log. Just as she wasn't drawn to photographing people, she also didn't normally have much interest in capturing wildlife with her camera; she preferred the emotions evoked by a landscape to the anthropomorphized poses of animals shared on social media. But the bird's silhouette was perfectly mirrored in the water, its majestic wings open wide, about to take flight. These commanding creatures were the closest thing to a dinosaur that Helene imagined she would ever encounter.

And then, like a tickle in the corner of her eye, Helene spotted a familiar pattern. A forest green and golden yellow checked scarf waving into the frame of the heron photograph, but the face of the person wearing the woollen accessory was just outside the shot.

Scrambling to grab her computer mouse, Helene shifted backwards and forwards through the photographs that were taken on the same day. Her immediate efforts were frustrated as Helene had taken no other images of the heron. She cursed herself for not following the journalism principle of always taking a backup shot. It wasn't until she clicked on a photo at the end of the breakwater, a view of the lighthouse with sun-frosted waves in the background, that her quarry was revealed: standing in profile, a woman with dark hair and the distinctive scarf, stared at the ocean in concentration, as though the deep waters held a message meant just for her.

Helene grabbed the cell phone off her desk, headed to the boardroom and closed the door behind her. Her imminent actions might be crossing a line as a journalist, but she still thought it was the right thing to do.

"What is it now?" the voice answered, this time with more than a hint of exasperation. The journalist could only assume Detective Kalinowski had caller ID, since she knew it was Helene on the phone. "I already told you I can't tell you anything, even if I had anything to tell."

Helene was unfazed by the officer's reaction. Journalists were trained to ignore the irritation of others — pissing people off was a sign you were doing the job right. "I have a photo. Of the woman. The dead one, I mean, obviously."

"You what?" Kalinowski asked, her annoyance replaced with cautious excitement.

"I walk on the breakwater every day. Sometimes in the morning, but mostly in the evening. It's a ritual, a routine, maybe a kind of therapy, even." Helene felt like she was telling the detective things she didn't need to know, but she was also aware that some kind of explanation for her fortuitous discovery was necessary. "Anyways, I take photos. Mostly of the sky and sunsets, but sometimes people too — people like me who visit regularly. And I found a photo of her . . . well, her scarf, really. But she is the one wearing the scarf."

After a moment of silence, Kalinowski stated, "I'm a little confused. Why are you doing this? Sharing information with the police, that is."

"I know. It feels weird for me too. And I will only send you this photo if you promise not to tell anyone how you got it. Journalists have a reputation to keep up — of being the nemesis of the police. I can't have this getting out."

"I don't really make promises to journalists. But you still haven't explained why you're giving the photo to me," said the detective, which Helene thought was a fair statement. She had already asked herself why she felt compelled to offer information.

"Because I found her, the woman, in the water. And it was awful. And now she is in my head. And I feel like she isn't going to get out of my head until I figure out what happened to her." *Like some kind of responsibility to the dead,* Helene almost added.

"And that's it?" Kalinowski's voice was thick with skepticism.

Helene said yes, although she knew there was more to it. Years of journalism, of reporting the murder and rape of women, and even sometimes children, had left her with a paralyzing sense of helplessness and hopelessness, as if there was nothing she could do but bear witness to the cruel grist mill that relentlessly churned life into death. Her role as

18

a journalist was to simply interview the survivors whose lives have been shattered by violence.

So, despite the questionable ethics of giving information to the police, Helene wanted to finally play a role in solving one of the crimes she had come across in her career. However, Helene's offering included another request.

"I'm obviously going to send you the photograph, for you to share with the public, but I do have a favour to ask," Helene said.

"And what's that?" The detective sounded as though her doubts about the journalist were about to be confirmed.

"That when you have a name for the woman, I am the first person in the media you tell. Just to get ahead of the pack."

"Well, that would be highly unethical," replied Kalinowski without sounding particularly concerned. "Let me see the photo and then we can talk."

Helene knew she didn't have the heart to negotiate, but she also suspected that Kalinowski was more appreciative than she was letting on. And getting on the right side of someone who could give you exclusive information was how good journalists uncovered great stories.

Chapter 4

Standing in a room full of people dressed in muted colours, Helene realized that memorial services were one event where introverts could be quite comfortable. If you wanted to sit quietly gazing out the window, no one would give you a hard time. The volume of voices was also usually kept to an acceptable hum. And there was a serenity and solemnity to the whole event generally absent from modern society — an existence many spent trying to imitate the hairstyle of a celebrity while labouring like an indentured servant to pay the mortgage.

Before leaving the house to attend a memorial for the dead woman, Helene had made two different dinners for her children, as they both had specific diets due to life-threatening food allergies. Her son, Oscar, was anaphylactic to dairy and bananas while her daughter, Cleo, could not eat any nuts or pitted fruits. Helene was grateful that her fourteen-year-old girl could now help prepare meals, cheerfully chopping cucumbers into animal shapes for her younger brother. The assistance she provided by folding laundry and unloading the dishwasher brought the first relief Helene had known from the endless domestic drudgery of being a single mother. Her son, who had turned ten that summer, would put away his folded pants, shirts and pyjamas, although usually in the wrong drawers, offering the kind of help that ultimately created more work for a parent.

Even though Helene had spent forty-five minutes in the kitchen that evening, she had arrived at the memorial hungry. Neither the grilled cheese sandwich for her daughter, nor the fried hot dogs for her son, had held any appeal. She was relieved to discover a generous spread of finger foods at the service, although the sausage rolls and sponge cake possessed more starch and echoes of British colonialism than she preferred. But in a town named after Queen Victoria, this kind of fare was still a staple.

Removing the face mask she sometimes wore for COVID protection, Helene picked up one of the smaller sausage rolls and took a bite of the greasy offering. Being a parent, she appreciated any food not cooked by herself. And, like other journalists, she would triple check the veracity of information for a news story and yet snack on day-old donuts of questionable provenance.

While chewing on the meaty, doughy pastry, Helene examined the numerous paintings hanging on the walls of the room where the service was being held. It was in fact the main gallery of the Amelia Grayson Museum, the former home of a 19th century landscape painter who had lived in James Bay. The artist's house had become not just a legacy of her work but of her life, with Victorian teapots and fire screens still in place. Due to the age of the wooden building and the mouldering wallpaper and carpets, the rooms were incredibly musty. Helene had once brought her allergic children on a tour, but they had to leave after a few minutes when they both started violently sneezing.

An immigrant from Northern England, Grayson had depicted verdant landscapes of Vancouver Island with vivid splashes of colour and shapes that were somewhere on the spectrum between realism and impressionism. And it was not just her boundary-pushing artwork that remained celebrated more than a century later, but also her unconventional life. Before the age of twenty, she had been put on an ocean liner to Canada, having been promised in marriage to a local timber baron. However, after arriving in her new country she decided against matrimony, living off a small inheritance and supplementing her income by doing commissioned portraits for wealthy families. Her body of work was limited as she had disappeared in her early

21

thirties. A shawl found on a beach led searchers to conclude the artist had drowned off the shores of her James Bay neighbourhood. More than one hundred years later, the mystery surrounding her demise persisted as no remains were ever discovered. It was never clearly established whether her death was by suicide, misadventure, or if foul play was involved.

The squeal of a microphone being turned on brought Helene back to the 21st century and the fact that she was investigating a more recent death, one which had clear indications of being a homicide.

After Helene had sent Detective Kalinowski her photos of the victim from the breakwater and they had been shared with the city's media, it had only been a matter of days before a member of the public came forward with an identification. The dead body belonged to a young woman named Lucy Marino, the head curator at the Amelia Grayson Museum. The woman had been on holiday leave at the time of her death, which explained why she had not been reported missing. And that evening, the museum staff were holding a memorial ceremony for their colleague who had come to such a violent end.

While several of the organizers continued to struggle with the sound system, Helene felt someone nudge her elbow, almost spilling the crumbs of the sausage roll from her napkin.

"Shouldn't you give them a hand? Being a radio girl and all. Aren't microphones kind of your thing?"

Turning in the direction of the teasing voice, Helene flashed an amused smile at Alex Chang, a writer for the local newspaper and long-time friend.

"You know technology is not really my thing. I'm all about the words," replied Helene.

"Well, if you're about words, you need to switch teams and work for my paper," answered Alex, engaging in a familiar debate between the two journalists. The writer was wearing a long grey trench coat and jeans that stopped short of her ankles. Her thick black hair had been pulled back into a cheerful ponytail, which belied her tenacious investigative instinct.

"What, you want more reporters chasing after the few jobs there are left in the newspaper industry? I'm amazed you're still printing a paper every day."

Alex laughed. "Oh, it's all about posting stories online, as you well know. And just yesterday I gained two more followers."

"Does that bring the total to a dozen?"

"Hey, my posts get at least ten likes each, even if they're only when I retweet the pet photo of the day."

"Yes, we are both in the wrong industry. We should be shooting cat videos."

"But where would be the thrill in that?" asked Alex. "I mean look at us now, attending the funeral of a dead curator of a dead artist. Doesn't get more exciting than that."

"Well, I for one will take murder over working with a furry mutt any day."

"Murder?" Alex injected a pause in their playful exchange. "Who said anything about murder?"

Helene realized that Alex had been working her craft, using their friendly chatter to lull Helene into dropping her guard and sharing a piece of information she had been trying to keep to herself. Friendship didn't make Helene out of bounds as a source. However, the radio journalist was spared from having to respond to her friend's query when the staff at the museum finally got the microphone working.

"We are here this evening to celebrate the life of our incredible colleague, Lucy Marino." A middle-aged woman wearing a shapeless beige dress and sporting a lopsided haircut leaned into the microphone which hadn't been raised to her height. Helene resisted the urge to jump onto the stage and make the adjustment. Her radio technical skills did go as far as making sure the position of a microphone allowed people to talk comfortably.

"Lucy Marino was a gifted curator who brought much needed attention and, if we are honest, funds to the museum. She also recently managed to secure two previously unknown Amelia Grayson paintings. These artworks will soon be revealed to the public at an unparalleled exhibition, an exhibition Lucy spent countless hours organizing in the days and weeks before her untimely death."

Taking a sip of grapefruit-flavoured fizzy water, Helene wondered if anyone else noticed that the eulogy to Lucy Marino was focused on money and art. So far, there had been no reference to the woman being a good friend or even a likeable human. But some people's identities were enmeshed in their jobs, and perhaps this was the case with the dead curator.

"We have placed a memorial book next to the front door, and you are welcome to share thoughts and condolences. The family has asked that donations be made to the Amelia Grayson Museum because that is what Lucy would have wanted. Thank you again for coming."

Triggering another high-pitched electronic squeal, the woman in the beige dress turned off the microphone. It was the shortest eulogy Helene had ever witnessed, but she knew that not everyone was inclined to deliver florid speeches. However, there had also been no opening for anyone else to come up on stage to share memories of Lucy, which made the service almost embarrassingly brief. Surveying the room, Helene noticed that no one looked particularly upset or sad, and there was even a small crowd who seemed to be restarting a jovial conversation.

"So, what were you saying about murder?" Alex hadn't missed a beat before turning her attention back to her friend.

"Just a minute," Helene said, placing her crumb-filled napkin and plastic cup of fizzy water on the table. "I need the bathroom. Bladder the size of a thimble!"

Making her escape before Alex could protest, Helene went down a hallway lined with several antique side tables holding tasteful bouquets of wildflowers, passed through a doorway made for people much shorter in stature, and finally arrived in a vestibule crowded with coats. A tall mahogany pedestal stood near the door, on which was resting the memorial book and pen. Looking around to see if anyone was watching, Helene was relieved to discover she was alone.

The leather book was opened to a page filled with notes of various and vague condolences. Most were expressing sympathy for the family rather than any sadness over the loss of a friend or colleague. Curious to see if she could find a comment that was more substantive or enlightening, Helene turned back one page in the book.

Her shock at the sight of the angry red letters scrawled across the page, almost like a bloodstain, caused Helene to come close to knocking over the pedestal. The journalist instinctively reached for her cell phone and took a photo of the book, which had been violated with one word: BITCH.

"Well, somebody isn't heartbroken that Marino is dead."

Helene once again didn't hear her friend sneaking up from behind. She made a mental note to buy Alex a cowbell so she would be warned of her approach.

"Apparently not," replied Helene, while wondering if she should rip out the offensive page to spare the family any additional pain. But she decided that since there was a murder investigation underway, such a move might be tantamount to destroying evidence. She knew she was going to have to send detective Kalinowski her photo.

"Murder and nasty notes — I feel like there is more to this story than a curator who went to the great museum in the sky before her time," said Alex. "What exactly aren't you telling me?"

"I found the body," Helene blurted out in response. She didn't exactly know why she was telling this to her friend, who was also her competitor. All she knew was that it felt good to share the burden.

Alex's eyes grew wide and then narrowed again.

"I think this is an occasion that requires more than carbonated fruit water. I'm taking you to the Empress Hotel for a shot of medicinal whisky." Alex nodded in the direction of a dramatic painting hanging on the wall, waves reflecting an amber sunset. "Amelia Grayson herself would approve, I heard she drew inspiration from a teacup of gin in the afternoon. A dislike of marriage, a fondness for booze. She was a woman after my own heart."

"That actually sounds pretty good," responded Helene, thinking that a strong drink might also wash away the greasy film in her mouth that was left behind from the sausage roll. "But I do still have to pee."

While her friend remained standing in the vestibule, Helene went back down the hallway to where the bathrooms were located. Opening the door, she was relieved to discover modern facilities, including two stalls and shiny fixtures. Helene could appreciate paintings from the 19th century, but plumbing was another matter entirely.

Locking the door on the first stall, Helene was in the process of undoing her belt when she heard another person enter the room. The journalist assumed the woman was talking to someone on a cell phone, as her urgent whispers echoed off the walls and tiled floors. The conversation continued as the woman stepped into the neighbouring stall. Helene remained standing as she eavesdropped on the conversation.

"I had to come. I mean, it would have looked bad if no one from the family had shown up."

Helene heard the bustle of the woman wrestling with her clothing and sitting down on the toilet. From under the stall divider, Helene spied a pair of worn brown ankle boots. "Don't worry, I'm getting the hell out of here now. I've done my duty. More than my duty. She doesn't deserve my tears after stealing the house. And you know what? At the end of the day, I'm glad she's dead."

Still listening from her own stall, Helene was disturbed to discover more evidence that the curator was not being particularly mourned. The woman then ended her call and flushed the toilet.

Rushing to open her own stall door, hoping to get a look at the other woman, Helene knocked over her expensive leather purse, which was overstuffed with notebooks, pens and a water bottle. As she scrambled to shove her belongings back into the bag, cursing herself for not using her regular practical backpack, Helene heard the woman wash her hands and leave the room. By the time the journalist managed to extricate herself from the stall and rush out of the bathroom, the hallway was empty.

When Helene passed under the low doorway to join Alex in the vestibule again, she stopped short. There were two additional people in the space, her friend standing to one side, trying to be as unobtrusive as the paintings on the wall.

"Thank you for joining us today to honour your sister. It means so much that you were here." The museum staff member with the lopsided hair was grasping both hands of another woman who looked distinctly uncomfortable.

The second figure was stout in stature and sported a brutally short haircut and denim overalls more suited to a workshop than a memorial service.

"Of course, and I'm grateful for the gathering," replied the woman without sounding grateful at all. "But I really must get going. So many things to arrange."

"I understand," the woman from the museum said, finally releasing the hands of the family member. "But you must take the memorial book with you, as a way to remember how much your sister meant to us."

The woman with the short hair picked up the weighty leather book with reluctance. She then turned around and marched out the front door, but not before Helene saw that she was wearing brown ankle boots — the ones the journalist had spied under the bathroom stall. The museum staff member left the vestibule as well but headed in the other direction.

"Are you ready to go?" Alex asked Helene once they were alone again.

"Sure," the journalist responded, while wondering how the woman she now believed was the curator's sister would react to the angry message the memorial book contained. Maybe not that badly considering her own evident animosity toward her sibling.

When Helene's thoughts returned to the present, she shared a wry smile with her friend. "Would you believe I still haven't peed?"

Chapter 5

Helene knew better than to trust the sun. Beaming brightly on the coastal James Bay neighbourhood, the glowing orb made the day appear welcoming and warm. A flock of robins, trilling and darting from budding branches to dewy grass, added to the appeal of the outdoors. But a chill wind blew across the ribbon of water separating the tip of Vancouver Island from Washington State, giving the air on that bright day a frosty sting. Before leaving home, Helene pulled on her knitted cap and gloves, wishing the summer would make an early appearance.

On weekdays, Helene visited the breakwater in the evening, her mornings too busy with shoving food into lunch bags and children out the door. But on the weekends, she liked to take photographs in the early light, when most of the world was still in bed. And she did feel a kindred connection to the other morning walkers who occasionally nodded politely in her direction, as though they were members of a secret club that prohibited all talking.

But on this morning, any meditative benefits of her oceanside promenade were marred by the company of another. After she had emailed Detective Kalinowski the photo of the memorial book, documenting the hateful word scrawled across a page, the police officer had wanted to discuss more details of the memorial for the curator. She said Helene could come down to the police station or they could meet somewhere else. The journalist decided being on familiar turf would be an advantage, as though she was a criminal who needed an edge.

Kalinowski was waiting at the start of the breakwater path, standing on the sundial etched into the ground, a takeout coffee cup in her hand. Clearly, she didn't understand Helene liked to move at a brisk pace, which made no allowance for the drinking of beverages.

"So, who else was at the museum?" asked the detective a few minutes later while stopping to take another sip of her coffee. Helene tried to hide her irritation at the slow progress they were making.

"Well, besides the sister and the museum staff, not many. I suppose there were a couple of people standing alone who might have been friends." Helene found no reason to mention that Alex, her fellow journalist, had been in attendance.

"No men?"

Helene paused before answering, going through her memories of the event like she was scanning photos on social media.

"That's funny, I didn't even notice, but now that you ask, there weren't any men. Well, maybe there was one young man putting out food on the tables, and another brought in some flowers. But otherwise, it was mostly female art enthusiasts of a certain age."

"Sounds very Victoria," scoffed Kalinowski.

"It was," agreed Helene. "Right down to the tea caddy. But why are you asking about men? Do you have a suspect?"

The detective shook her head. "It's just a matter of statistics. When women are the victims of violence, it's usually at the hands of men. Women shooting women isn't really a thing."

"I suppose that's fair," mused the journalist, unable to recall any news stories containing that kind of scenario.

"There was something very strange, however, discovered by the coroner."

"Oh, yes?" replied Helene with curiosity. "And you are going to share it with me?"

30

The elegant detective, whose hair was free from tangles despite the morning wind, smiled mischievously at Helene. "I believe we are in a position of mutually assured destruction."

Helene tilted her head to the side, slightly perplexed. She was not sure how a term used to describe the Cold War truce between the US and Russia could be applied to their fledgling relationship.

"You shared photos with the police. Not strictly something a journalist is meant to do. But it really kick-started the investigation. So, in return, I am going to disclose a piece of information to you, mostly because I have no idea what it means, and I hope you can help. I also figure you won't tell on me because then I would tell on you."

Helene appreciated the detective's ability to move from metaphors involving nuclear rivals to the social dynamics of schoolchildren.

"To start off, there was no bullet in the body, so we can't use that to trace the weapon. That's a big setback for us. However, inside the wound, the coroner discovered the strangest deposits — traces of dandelion."

"Like the garden weed?" asked Helene in confusion.

"That's the only kind of dandelion I know of."

"Dandelion. But it's the beginning of March. Dandelions don't even bloom for another month."

"I know," replied the detective. Evidently, she had already taken the seasons into consideration.

"Well, that is really odd," was all the response that Helene could offer.

The two women had halted their progress on the breakwater, giving Helene a chance to ponder this new information. She was so deep in thought she almost didn't notice the Coast Guard boat slipping by in the water. Jeff was at the helm, steering past the other boats in the harbour. Lee, who was standing on the outer deck, raised a hand in Helene's direction — not so much a friendly wave, but a mark of recognition.

"We had to test everyone at the scene for gunshot residue," stated the detective, nodding in the direction of the boat. "Came back negative."

"That seems a bit of a stretch — a Coast Guard officer rushing to the scene of their own crime?"

"An officer who was in the vicinity at the time of the body's discovery, and knows the area, can't be written off as a suspect," replied Kalinowski without apology.

Helene looked at the other woman directly. "But that would have been the worst planned murder in history, to leave a body where you work. And surely if you were a Coast Guard officer, there would be better places to hide a body, like the middle of the ocean."

"That is a valid observation. But we still have to eliminate people from our inquiries. Just part of the process." The detective took another sip of her coffee and surveyed the view from the breakwater. "I have to say, it's an awfully pretty place for a murder."

Helene wanted to comment that she was trying her best to disassociate the crime from her daily pilgrimage, and that the detective wasn't helping. Not to mention they were doing much more talking than walking.

Then the journalist suddenly realized where she was on the breakwater — the same spot from which she had spied the body just over a week ago. Peering over the edge of the railing with trepidation, as though another dead woman might be floating below, she was relieved to see nothing more than water and speckled stone. The journalist wasn't sure whether to envy or distrust the ocean for its indifference to death. Sparkling, blithesome waves now splashing across the scene of the crime.

"What was the sister like?" asked the detective. "At the memorial service."

"Kind of all over the map," replied Helene, pulling herself back from the railing. "She seemed angry, like someone who had been hurt, but also as if her pain had made her stronger, tougher. She also appeared to be very practical. Sturdy footwear, no-nonsense hair. Not like someone whose sister had dedicated themselves to art. I don't know if that's helpful or just confusing." Helene looked at the detective to see if she was going to dismiss her random observations, but Kalinowski nodded thoughtfully.

"Sounds like the two sisters were chalk and cheese."

"Yes, there was a lot of that there too."

"What?"

"Cheese," joked Helene. "And sausage rolls." She was about to apologize for her weak attempt at humour but was interrupted by the sound of her cell phone ringing.

"Just a second, it might be my kids. I have to answer in case it's an emergency." Her children's anaphylactic allergies meant that every phone call could be the start of a harrowing trip to the emergency room.

"Hey, Helene! How's it going?"

At the sound of her friend Alex's voice, the journalist could feel her nervous system slam the brakes on her racing heart and mind. No hospital trip today. No wrestling with mute gods over the fate of the ones she loved more than life.

"I'm okay. Just out on the breakwater. What's up?" Helene didn't want to mention she was starting her weekend by going for a walk in the company of a police officer.

"Oh, right — nature, exercise. Don't quite get it. But you know, whatever turns your crank."

Helene knew her friend's idea of spending time out of doors was raising a martini glass on a restaurant patio. She was a true journalist when it came to her health regimen.

"Anyway, I called because I tracked down the sister from the memorial. Her name is Paola Marino, and she

33

owns a bakery," stated Alex. "Gluten-free. Might check out their biscotti."

"You what?" Helene asked in a voice louder than intended. Alex hadn't mentioned she was going to start investigating people connected to the murder. Detective Kalinowski gave the journalist a look of curiosity.

"Yes, it's called Morning Glory Bakery. Up on Fort Street."

With forced levity, Helene replied, "That's great. I can't wait to see the photos of the juvenile orca. Sounds like you got a great shot."

"Juvenile orca? What? Oh . . . I get it. You can't talk right now." Alex's tone then switched from understanding to suspicious. "Who are you with? What's going on? Don't forget, you said we were going to work together on this. At least that's what you agreed to after a few drinks at the Empress."

Helene realized she might need to clarify what exactly *working together* meant. She certainly hadn't expected her friend to track down the workplaces of possible murder suspects without checking with her first. But that conversation would have to wait until she wasn't standing next to a police officer.

Wanting to wrap up the call, Helene stated, "You have a video of the orca pod too? Fabulous. You can just text everything to my cell."

"Alright, don't overdo it. I'll send you the address for the bakery. Call me back when you can."

Helene put the phone in her pocket, wondering if she was going to regret inviting her friend to help investigate the murder.

Turning to the detective, she said, "Sorry about that. Some paddle-boarder has spotted what he believes is a young orca off Galiano Island. Good news for the pod but also great clickbait for the station."

"Funny, it sounded like you were talking to a friend when you answered," said Kalinowski.

"Oh, I like to keep things casual. Makes people more relaxed and willing to share their story."

"That's a bit manipulative."

"And you don't manipulate people in your line of work?" countered Helene.

"Yes, but I am trying to bring criminals to justice."

Glancing down at the watery scene of the crime, Helene thought, *You aren't the only one.*

Then, out loud, Helene asked in a straightforward manner, "Are we done now? I would love to take some photos. The sun is dancing on the waves this morning." Helene wanted to get away from the detective before she had to deliver any more lies.

"Sure," the detective answered. "If I have more questions, I know where to find you."

The detective walked on ahead without Helene, choosing to make the journey to the lighthouse at the end of the breakwater before returning. It was a natural human instinct — to follow the path as far as it would go.

As Helene focused her camera on the water, trying to capture the luminous, undulating patterns with her lens while avoiding the exact spot where the body had floated, she mulled over the conversations she had just had with the detective and her friend.

Was the sister a possible suspect in the murder of the curator?

Was a man responsible for the brutal violence?

Why were there traces of dandelion in the gunshot wound?

Eventually, Helene's questions about Lucy Marino's murder ebbed away into silence as the kaleidoscope of sunlight on the ocean washed away all other thoughts — beauty once again proving it was more compelling than death.

Chapter 6

During the month of March, many of the streets in Victoria could be mistaken for the adorned archways of an excessively sentimental wedding ceremony, as though decorated under the orders of a tyrannical bride who could pull strings with Mother Nature. Both cherry and plum trees exploded in blossoms of infinite shades of pink, confetti composed of petals sweeping across sidewalks and nestling against curbs. Helene lived a few blocks from South Turner Street in James Bay, one of the most blushing blocks in the entire city. And although it was out of her way to drive along the road, the visual symphony of coral and rose, like a sunset that lasted for weeks, was worth the short detour.

After Helene's eyes had taken in the beauty of the blossom-lined streets on the Monday-morning commute, the next to be indulged were her olfactory senses. Pulling open the front door of the Morning Glory bakery, Helene was met by a waft of air infused with cinnamon and chocolate. Sleek glass shelves displayed cakes, oversized cookies, and a variety of muffins for those interested in a slightly healthier fare. There were already four people waiting in line to be served, a testament to the popularity of the shop.

Helene had decided to follow up on her friend's discovery of the bakery owned by the sister of the dead curator. On first entering the store, she didn't immediately see the woman from the memorial working behind the counter, so she decided to join the queue. If nothing else, she could always buy a dozen cookies to bring back to the newsroom. Not even a leaked government document on the misuse of public funds excited journalists as much as a box of sugar and carbohydrates first thing in the morning.

"Just a second, I'll check for you. I think she's in her office."

Helene had made it to the front of the line, and after buying half a dozen cookies for her colleagues, she asked if the owner was around. When the staff member disappeared through the doorway to look in the back, an older woman standing behind the journalist huffed with impatience at the delay in service. Helene was always impressed by how quickly people became irritated by minor inconveniences in Victoria. Reading about the lives of children in refugee camps as part of her job kept most of her minor complaints in check.

"Come on through," said the young man in a white apron when he returned. "It's the room to the right in the back. Says she has a minute to spare."

After putting her cookies into her backpack, hoping they wouldn't get crushed, Helene followed the bakery worker through the connecting doorway. She passed by stacks of oversized sacks containing gluten-free flour that resembled sandbags used to prevent homes from flooding during a recent storm Helene had covered for the news. There were also pre-formed cardboard boxes in a range of sizes waiting to be filled with baked goods. They all bore the stamp of the bakery's Morning Glory logo, which was written in cursive lettering over a rising sun. Helene wondered if she would have anything in common with the gruff-looking sister other than an appreciation for an early start to the day.

"Before you even ask, we don't do substitutions for eggs or dairy. We aren't a vegan bakery. Just gluten-free."

When Helene had been shown through to a cramped office on the far side of the kitchen, Lucy Marino's sister didn't even look up from a desk covered in papers before making a statement meant to cut off requests from demanding customers.

37

"Oh, I'm not here about ingredients," replied Helene, although normally asking questions about allergens was exactly what she would be doing in a bakery.

"Well, that's a first," said the woman, who then looked up from the paperwork and asked, "What do you want?"

As a journalist, Helene believed in getting straight to the point, even when dealing with sensitive matters. Most people who were grieving seemed to appreciate the directness. While friends and family avoided the awkward conversations around death, for reporters it was just part of the job.

"My name is Helene, and I'm a journalist. I have been following the death of your sister."

"Really?" the baker responded with incredulity, evidently surprised that her dead sibling would garner this attention.

"I'd like to do a short radio piece about her life and her work as a curator — paint a picture of her legacy, as it were." Helene offered a sympathetic smile, but she wasn't prepared for the reaction her explanation received: the baker had doubled over with laughter.

"Her legacy?" the sister finally managed to say after catching her breath. "Lucy would have loved that. She really would." Once she stopped gasping for air, she looked at Helene with more than a hint of scepticism. "You're writing a story about a failed artist who became a curator of a bunch of old paintings of trees?"

Although Helene was not an art expert, she bristled at the description of Amelia Grayson's work. But she knew starting an argument about the artist's legacy was not going to endear her to the sister.

"It's important the media reflects the local community and takes the time to celebrate the lives of those who have made contributions," she said, hoping she sounded more convincing than she felt. Taking a notebook from her pocket, she then decided the best defence was an offence — it was

38

time to get a few answers out of the sister who couldn't cook up a little sorrow for a lost sibling.

"You say Lucy was an artist. Did she paint?" asked Helene. "And, just to confirm, your name is Paola — Paola Marino?"

"You want to do this now?" The sister responded to Helene's question with her own, but then, with a heavy sigh, she turned away from the messy desk. "Okay, why not?" She motioned for Helene to sit in a chair in the corner of the cramped room. "Yes, I'm Paola."

Without more prompting, the baker began to talk. "You asked if she was a painter, and yes, she always was. Even as a child. Growing up, she was treated like a little genius. At home, at school, adults always fawning over her." Paola spoke with jealousy that had been seasoned over time. "My mother even put her paintings in fancy frames we couldn't afford, and then hung them in the living room. They were the kind of things a kid would paint — pink flowers and raccoons with big eyes. But the worst was when my mom's friends came over for drinks, she would get Lucy to do a sketch of them — as a sort of party trick. She'd even haul her out of bed sometimes. It really wasn't pleasant. My mom was a big fan of old Scotch and new men." For the first time, Paola was expressing something approximating sadness when talking about her dead sister.

Now that the words were flowing, Helene sensed that Paola would need little encouragement. Unlike what the general public believed — that journalists hounded people to tell their stories — most individuals who had been through trauma wanted to share their experience. Helene thought it could be cathartic, even healing. And yet she knew journalists also had a responsibility not to take advantage of people when they were most vulnerable.

Paola started to tug on the loose strings at the frayed edges of her apron while she continued her story, as though trying to untangle the knot of loss and resentment in her heart.

"Of course, she ended up going to art college. Everyone knew she would. And as always, she was the star of her class — at least in the beginning. Nominated for awards, her professors taking special notice. In her first year, she was even invited to have a piece included in a show for older students. My mom made such a fuss about that. But then something went wrong. This was all before we had much money, before my mother had the wisdom to marry someone who had a bit of cash in the bank and a big house with a yard."

A knock on the office door interrupted the sister's recollection. A tall woman who looked improbably thin for someone who worked with sugar and starch all day stuck her head around the corner.

"Sorry," the woman said apologetically. "We can't get the second oven to heat up."

"Dammit," swore Paola. "Must be the bottom element again. I've got to go deal with this. We have a big wedding order to get ready."

Helene tried to hide her frustration. "Can you just tell me how your sister became a curator?"

"Honestly, I'm not sure. Isn't that what most failed artists do?" The sister stood up to leave the room. "All I know is that the job clearly paid better than I would have thought. She bought a new Audi last month." After a short pause, she added, "But maybe she was just burning through the inheritance."

"What inheritance?" asked Helene, trying to keep the conversation going.

"The one she stole from me after my mom died. The house, the bank account. Everything our new 'dad' left behind when he had a heart attack. I'm not surprised he didn't last long. My mother was a handful. Like my sister. Two peas in a pod. That's why Lucy was the favourite child.

40

How she convinced my mom to leave her the lot." Paola made the statement flatly and then strode out of the room.

Sighing heavily, Helene accepted she had gotten all the information she could out of the sister that day, but the journalist also knew she wasn't leaving empty-handed. Questions had been raised in her mind about money and jealousy, two very strong motives for murder. However, while shoving the notebook into her backpack, Helene did wonder if the fact that Paola couldn't be bothered to hide her animosity toward her sister meant she wasn't guilty of murder. Or was it to put her off the scent?

Making her way past trays and boxes to the exit, she could hear the baker yelling in frustration.

"I know we need a new oven, but where exactly am I supposed to get the money? It's going to take months to sell my mother's house even once it comes to me. I will just have to get it working again somehow. Try banging on the side like you did last time."

Clearly Paola expected to inherit her mother's property in the wake of her sister's death. And the loud kitchen discussion only confirmed for Helene that money could have been a motive for murder. The journalist made a note to check the details of the mother's will. As long as it had gone to probate it would be part of the public record. It was unlikely the curator had made her own will as people under forty rarely did, since they planned to live forever.

The journalist was distracted with thoughts of sibling rivalry as she slipped between the glass counters on her way out of the bakery. Glancing down, she noticed some curious-looking cookies, each one decorated with what looked like a purple pansy, the flower petals delicately pressed down into the dough before baking. While she was admiring the unique culinary creations, the sister came to stand next to her.

"When will the article come out?" she demanded.

"What article?" replied Helene absently, still examining the cookies on display.

"The one you're writing about Lucy." Paola eyed the journalist with distrust.

"It's actually for the radio, not a paper, but maybe I will have a chance to write something up online as well." People often assumed her work was for print. Newspapers were perceived as more substantial than the ephemeral voices on the radio. A broadcast was transitory like a sunset, although podcasts of programs, just like photos of sunsets, made a permanent record of the impermanent.

"Hopefully it will be ready to go to air in a couple of days. I'll let you know." Switching the topic without much subtlety, Helene then asked, "Do you use other flowers in your baking?"

"Sometimes," the sister said. "They are a bit of an experiment."

"They're pretty. And delicious, I would guess."

Helene then left the shop without pressing the sister for more details of her floral ingredients, she didn't want to raise further suspicion. But while pulling out of the parking lot, she couldn't help but wonder whether the baker ever used dandelions in her kitchen. A weed that had bloomed during a season for murder.

Chapter 7

"Why does everyone in this family use my charging cord?" Oscar's complaint rang out across the kitchen at a volume Helene considered excessive for 7:30 AM. It was another weekday morning, and her children had transitioned from sleeping to bickering in less time than it took to make toast.

"Because you always leave your cord in the kitchen," replied Cleo, effortlessly blaming her brother for his own problems in the way only siblings can.

"Well, why don't they use your phone charger?" demanded Oscar.

"Because it's in my bedroom."

"But you say no one can go in there."

"I AM ENTITLED TO MY PRIVACY!"

Watching her daughter emphasize her self-righteous declaration by gesticulating with a cereal spoon, the journalist made a mental note that if she was ever accused of a crime, she would make sure to hire a teenager for a lawyer.

After visiting Paola Marino's bakery the previous morning, the rest of the workday in the newsroom had passed much like any other. She had been asked by her producer to follow up on a press release on a new housing project for vulnerable women, and that night she had a restless sleep full of dreams about having to live on the streets with her children. The next morning, she was grateful to wake in her own home but soon found herself once again slicing apples for lunch while her children slaughtered her nerves during breakfast.

43

"Enough with the charging cords!" Helene said. "You know, some kids don't have enough to eat, even on this island — they go to school hungry!"

Her outburst sparked a duet of groans from her children. If there was one thing that could unite arguing siblings, it was an annoying parent.

Cleo looked up at her mother and said, "It would be great if you could stop being a journalist for two seconds. No one can complain without you marching out a bigger tragedy. It's bad enough we have to listen to stories about death on the radio while eating breakfast. Don't you care about our mental health?"

With that comment from her daughter, Helene wondered if there was any weapon in the history of people hurting other people so pointed as the guilt delivered by a teenager to their parent. Admittedly, if the morning news was adapted into a movie, Helene would consider it too violent for her children to watch.

Trying to move on, Helene asked her daughter, "Did you like the pita bread I bought yesterday? It's the only one I could find without sesame in it." Her daughter had a mild allergy to the seed now found in most breads and seasonings. Helene had visited three different grocery stores to find the sesame-free product.

"Yes, it's pretty good," said Cleo, with a noncommittal shrug.

"Okay, great. I didn't want to get a second package in case it went stale. I really don't like to eat pita that is more than two days old."

"Well, maybe you can give it to the starving children of Vancouver Island! I am sure they aren't that picky," smirked Cleo before waltzing out of the kitchen in triumph.

Helene wasn't sure if it was an indication of excellent or awful parenting when children called out adult hypocrisy while still in their pyjamas.

Oscar then got up from the table and handed Helene his latest drawing of an orca that he had created between spoonfuls of cereal. The so-called killer whales were her son's favourite animals, which was a relief to the journalist as there was no chance she could offer one as a pet. She would add the pencil sketch of the finned mammal to the collection that already decorated her desk at work.

Miraculously, her son also put his bowl in the dishwasher and then gave his mom a hug before heading to his bedroom to change. At the age of ten, he was still incredibly affectionate, and Helene dreaded when puberty would reveal to him that parents were to be abhorred, not adored.

After dropping off her kids at school, checking first to make sure they had their epinephrine kits in their backpacks in case of a serious allergic reaction, Helene drove straight to Moss Bay City Hall instead of the office. The previous afternoon, she had managed to convince her boss to let her do a short obit about Lucy Marino, but she still had to keep up with her regular assignments. And today there was a special council meeting to look at a new parking bylaw which was sure to cause a collision between the generations.

Helene also planned to visit the Amelia Grayson Museum later that day to follow up on some questions raised during her conversation with Lucy's sister, the baker. But as she drove along the streets of the affluent Moss Bay neighbourhood, where even the trees looked prosperous with green foliage, she reminded herself that journalism was paying for her sesame-free pita bread, not her personal murder investigation.

Moss Bay was perched along the stunning west-facing beaches of Greater Victoria, allowing residents to enjoy their superlative sunrises while sipping their designer coffees. The architecture of the houses ranged from renovated brick homes built in the early 1900s to newly constructed mega-mansions with five bedrooms and six bathrooms and closets

45

the size of a downtown studio apartment but with better views.

A generous portion of the population was composed of retired baby boomers who had won life's lottery. In their younger years they had landed great jobs, and in their older years they were enjoying greater pensions. They had bought homes in the 1970s for $40,000 that were now worth close to $2,000,000. Their cars were electric, and their front yards were curated. The only thing missing from this well-appointed neighbourhood was any trace of compassion. Every attempt at low-income or sheltered housing in the community was met by petitions and opposition.

There were some families with children, and other folks who worked at places like the nearby hospital — people who still had to worry about the increasing price of gas and groceries and taking time off work to take their kids to the dentist. But when Helene walked into the packed city council room, she could see that a healthy number of residents had no other occupation besides defending the status quo of their wealthy community.

The issue up for discussion that morning was a motion brought forward by one of the city councillors to only allow a homeowner to park on the street in front of their house. This push for a sort of de facto control of the roadscape came after years of reports of nasty notes being left on car windshields. Helene had read some of these hand-scrawled messages and was impressed by the level of privilege they reflected — the homeowner outraged that they couldn't use the parking spot to unload groceries or relatives. This was despite the fact that most single-family homes in Moss Bay also had garages and driveways for off-street parking. What it seemed to boil down to was that residents were frustrated that it still wasn't 1982, when there were fewer people and cars. What they needed was not so much a new parking bylaw but a time machine.

To be fair, Moss Bay wasn't the only community on the southern tip of Vancouver Island struggling with congestion. Even in Helene's sleepy James Bay neighbourhood, mostly populated by seniors surviving on a more modest income, there was a throng of people at the local supermarket any time after 10 AM. Standing in the long lineups for the checkout, shoppers clutched their discounted chicken thighs while unsteadily pushing their aluminum walkers ahead, inch by inch. Outside the store, the parking lot was fraught with aggression as elderly drivers competed for spots. And if one aged motorist pulled ahead of another who had been waiting, they became angrier than when a dog peed on their favourite rhododendron bush.

Perhaps the greatest symptom of island overload was the state of the ferry system. Besides pricey helicopter and seaplane rides, most of the population got off and on the island by taking the massive ocean-going vessels. The journey involved lining up an hour ahead at the Swartz Bay docks, followed by an almost two-hour voyage to the Tsawwassen terminal, and then still another hour's drive to Vancouver, depending on the traffic. The expedition was a slog, but it was considered the price you paid not to live in the crowded chaos that was the mainland.

However, a journey by ferry, which in the past was considered a dependable nuisance, had become as unreliable as sunshine during an island spring. The cancellation of ferry sailings occurred on an almost-daily basis, especially on holiday weekends when there was an extra crush of travellers. Crew shortages were stated as the cause of the changes to the schedule, as the ferry service struggled to hire staff like so many other businesses on the island. It seemed that the community had too many people and not enough people at the same time.

Before trying to find a seat in the city hall boardroom, Helene retrieved a face mask from her backpack. The space was crowded enough for her to want to take COVID

47

precautions, although she suspected the mostly older folks around her were up to date with vaccinations. She then secured a chair at the end of a row, the better to escape the room if she received an urgent call from the newsroom.

"We acknowledge that the land on which we gather is the traditional territory of the Coast and Straits Salish Peoples. Specifically we recognize the Lekwungen peoples known today as the Songhees and Esquimalt Nations, and that their historic connections to these lands continue to this day."

The meeting began with the territorial acknowledgement for the Indigenous Peoples on whose lands the wealthy community was built. Helene wondered if she was the only one who realized this meeting was about the ownership of street parking on Indigenous territories. She sensed the irony was wasted on the room of outraged residents.

A microphone had been placed at the front of the room, and one speaker after another outlined the daily frustration of having the street in front of their house congested with cars. Although they talked about wanting to use the space themselves, for quick errands or for guests, Helene suspected their complaints were spurred by a sense that the world was becoming increasingly beyond their control. They had lived a life of privilege, and their opinions used to carry weight. But now they had been reduced to waiting endless hours on the phone for help with everything from online banking to their smart fridge that refused to make ice cubes. If they could once more assert dominion over the twenty feet of pavement in front of their house, it would feel like a victory.

No one spoke up against a possible change to street parking. Helene imagined that the younger folks who might want to leave their car in the nearest available spot had jobs that kept them from attending council meetings first thing on a weekday morning.

Helene tried to imagine what the Victorian-era painter Amelia Grayson would make of this parking dispute. When she strolled the dusty boardwalks of Victoria in the 1880s, there would have been no shortage of places to tie up a horse or carriage. Would she support the rights of landowners that aligned with the colonial legacy of her times? Despite her defiance of the dictates to marry and raise children, she came from a wealthy family. And the journalist found most people believed in social equality until the moment it threatened their own comfort.

An hour later, it came as no surprise that the meeting ended without any clear resolution. The parking issue was set to be reviewed by city staff who would come up with recommendations in the next six months — a strategy that gave the appearance of doing something while committing to nothing. Helene couldn't blame the councillors for hoping the issue would blow over, at least until the next election.

With a 12:30 newscast deadline looming, Helene drove straight to the office. It took her less than thirty minutes to file a story on the parking debate, having written most of the lines during the meeting. She only needed to pull a few audio clips of residents who had shared their concerns, as well as a reaction from the mayor. It wasn't exactly Pulitzer Prize-winning broadcasting, but it was the meat and potatoes of small-town journalism.

Once her story was filed, Helene made some vague comments about checking out a new rooftop garden at a senior's home and then slipped out of the office. Her producer Riya was busy on the phone, and she hadn't assigned the journalist any other stories for the day.

After a short drive, Helene pulled up in front of the Amelia Grayson Museum and took note that the street parking was reserved for residents. The parking wars were clearly not limited to the boundaries of Moss Bay. However, the journalist decided to run the risk of leaving her car in front of a small bungalow with drawn curtains, betting that the homeowner was away. The properties of many retirees in Victoria were left unoccupied during the winter months, the residents trading in the West Coast rain for the Mexican sun. Looking through her windshield at a monochrome sky of grey that promised a day of relentless drizzle, Helene couldn't blame them.

Just about to open the car door and cross the street to the museum, Helene froze at the sight of Detective Kalinowski exiting the building. Instinctively, she hunched down in her front seat until the officer had gotten into her own vehicle and driven off.

Helene wasn't sure why she had hidden from the detective — she had already chartered questionable ethical territory by sharing the breakwater photos of Lucy Marino with the police. Maybe it was just a sense of guilt for meddling where she strictly shouldn't, but that only demonstrated that she was in the right career. Being nosy was a job requirement for journalism.

Chapter 8

Standing in the museum front entrance, Helene took a moment to listen for the heavy footfall of any stray police officers remaining in the building. She tried to calm her nerves with the thought that no one but Kalinowski would recognize her, and the research she was doing for Marino's obit could be offered as an excuse for loitering on the premises. Thankfully, there wasn't anyone minding the admission desk. Perhaps the island labour shortage included museum volunteers.

After peeking around the corner into a silent gallery off the vestibule, she made her way down the musty main hallway, at the end of which she discovered a staircase leading to an upper floor. The passage was roped off, and a sign indicated that it was for staff only. However, Helene had long interpreted attempts to restrict access as merely suggestions to be mostly ignored.

Glancing up at the winding staircase, the journalist was more concerned about the structural integrity of the narrow passage and sloping steps. There wasn't even a handrail to hold onto. She wasn't sure if housing inspectors existed when Queen Victoria sat on the throne. The excess of death by poor sanitation during the 19th century made her think it was not a priority for the long-lived monarch.

The boards of the stairway groaned in protest as Helene made her ascent to the second floor, eliminating any chance of a stealthy approach. This is perhaps why, when she reached the top landing, a concerned face was peering around the corner of an office doorway along the upper hallway.

51

"Are you with the police? Did you forget something?" asked a woman with a large bun perched on top of her head like a misplaced breakfast roll. Her worn yellow cardigan fell open to reveal a faded floral blouse.

"Not exactly," responded Helene while moving down the hall. "I'm a journalist. I was hoping we could talk about Lucy."

"Oh, I'm just the archivist," the woman protested as she went back into the office and slipped behind a desk as if it offered some kind of protection. When Helene followed her into the room, she saw that the walls were lined with shelves holding labelled boxes, some identified by year, like 1882, and others by category such as PROPERTY HISTORY.

"You need to talk with Ivy. She is the executive director of the museum," the woman stated once she was sitting down, arranging a stapler and paper pad that were already tidy. Helene wondered if the archivist was referring to the woman with lopsided hair who had led the memorial service.

"It's nothing so formal," said the journalist, smiling, hoping to put the older staff member at ease. "I just want to get a sense of who she was. I'm doing a short obituary. I'm Helene Unger, by the way. With Vancouver Island Radio."

"Hana," replied the woman, too polite to refuse introducing herself. "But I honestly didn't know Lucy that well. She dealt with the paintings and organizing exhibitions. My work is to preserve the artifacts from Grayson's life, the records of her daily existence that reveal so much about the woman who was the artist." A spark of passion had entered the voice of the archivist as she explained a job that was clearly a calling.

Trying to stay on the topic of the dead curator, Helene enquired, "Do you know anything about Lucy's employment before she came to the museum? She must have had exceptional references to get this position."

The archivist couldn't resist a question that required a clarification of facts; it was like offering salmonberries to a

52

hungry bear. "Just give me a minute, the staff records are kept in another office down the hall."

Left alone in the cloistered room, Helene marvelled at the shelves of neat boxes that reached from the floor to the ceiling. Her own home was overwhelmed by the chaos of abandoned toys and mismatched plastic lunch containers. The only organizing the journalist managed these days was occasionally filling a garbage bag of old puzzles or dried-up clay — a feeble attempt to halt a tsunami of stuff from washing away any order to her life. And she was guilty of adding to the mess herself. The kitchen table was often littered with unopened mail and articles she had printed up for work.

When the archivist returned to the room, she clutched a file folder to her chest. "You said this was for an obituary in the paper?"

"A story about her for the radio," corrected Helene.

"Well, anything that will remind people of the work Lucy did to lift up Grayson's legacy," said the woman, more interested in bringing attention to the long-dead artist than to the recently murdered curator.

Opening the file on the table, the archivist scanned the documents. "It says here that she graduated from the Pacific Art Institute ten years ago with honours in Fine Arts but also a minor in art history. And then it seems she came to work for us a few years later." The curator paused thoughtfully and then added, "I must say that it is quite an achievement, going straight from college to becoming a curator. It actually seems a bit irregular."

This woman, whose purpose was to bring order to the world, was visibly flummoxed by this early and unusual career achievement by Lucy Marino. Helene didn't want to add to the archivist's concerns by sharing the sister's belief that the curator had dropped out of art school.

"Well, she was obviously good at her job. The museum seems to get lots of attention." Helene spoke with enthusiasm, not wanting to lose the momentum of the conversation. "And I heard mention at the memorial service that she had even discovered some unknown paintings by Grayson. Do you know where she found them?" Helene didn't have any reason to believe the artwork was connected to the murder of the curator, but it was a curiosity she couldn't help but explore.

The archivist shook her head. "Lucy would never reveal the source of the paintings. She claimed the collector who owned them didn't want any attention from the media. But the works went through a very rigorous testing process. The canvases, the frames, the paint even matches the chemistry of her other artworks." The archivist paused for a moment and then continued. "Funny, the police asked about the new paintings too."

"Oh," responded Helene calmly, trying to mask a frisson of excitement. "Did they think there was something questionable about them?"

"Not at all," replied the archivist with a note of indignation, like the integrity of the museum was in doubt. "They just wanted to go over all the aspects of Lucy's job and anything out of the ordinary."

"Of course," responded the journalist, trying to placate the archivist. "They must be worth a fortune, though."

"Their monetary value is irrelevant. What they add to the legacy of Grayson's talent is priceless. You see, it is profoundly rare for new paintings to come to light for any artist. It happened with Van Gogh, *Sunset at Montmajour.* He painted it just two years before his death. Quite the coup for the museum in Amsterdam."

"Did the police ask about anything else besides the paintings?" Helene hoped the woman wasn't put off by her numerous questions about the murder investigation.

"Just the usual things. How long she had been here. Any friction with the other employees. How much money she made, which seems a bit garish, if you ask me."

54

Love, lust and money. Helene was tempted to explain to the archivist that these were three top motives for murder.

"They seemed to imply she was spending a bit beyond her means. Which of course I could not comment on. I don't notice material objects like bags or expensive shoes. I am only interested in the things that bring true richness to life. Art, literature, the bouquet of a fine wine."

Helene considered pointing out that you needed money to enjoy simple but expensive pleasures like fine wine, but she didn't want to contradict the archivist, who had turned out to be quite helpful. The woman probably appreciated having company beyond the tidy stacks of boxes.

"They took some papers from Lucy's office, which I didn't strictly approve of. Although they did give me receipts for everything."

"Do you mind if I see her office?" Helene asked as casually as she could manage.

The archivist took a moment to respond. "I suppose. Just a look. Not to take anything."

"Of course," Helene reassured her.

The woman slipped past the desk, picking up a large ring of keys that could have been Victorian originals for the heft and size of them. Helene followed her down the wooden hallway with a floor that tilted slightly to the left. The archivist may have considered herself above the base lure of money, but the museum looked overdue for a list of repairs fuelled by cash.

At the end of a passage, the two women arrived at a door with a plaque that indicated it was the office of the late curator. The archivist sorted through the keys on the ring, selecting one with confidence despite their similar appearance. Once the door had been opened, Hana indicated she didn't want the journalist to cross the threshold. Helene imagined that, in the woman's mind, the objects in the office were no longer part of the present daily life, but artifacts from the dead curator's existence which now needed cataloguing.

Helene was disappointed to see that the office of Lucy Marino looked much like any other. Notepads, a lamp, an assortment of pens, all of which could have been the inspiration for a still-life painting of a desk. A wall calendar was the kind real estate companies gave away as gifts, with the March page revealing a photo of Victoria's Empress Hotel. Helene was admittedly surprised that a curator — especially one with a creative background — wouldn't have had more discriminating tastes in wall decor. The only thing which piqued her curiosity was a file cabinet with a half-opened drawer. But the journalist imagined the police had already plundered anything worth taking.

The archivist was facing the other direction down the hallway, like a watchdog in a cardigan, scanning for intruders, when Helene spotted a box in the corner of the tidy office bearing the label FOR SHREDDING. Moving swiftly, so Hana wouldn't notice, Helene lifted the lid and peeked inside. There were several stacks of identical pamphlets appearing to be a collection of letters written by Amelia Grayson.

Helene quickly slipped one of the pamphlets into her coat pocket and then let the curator know she was finished. After relocking the door, the archivist turned to Helene and enthusiastically asked, "Perhaps you would also like to view Grayson's studio?"

"Absolutely," Helene replied, wanting to keep the archivist happy. The pair walked halfway down the hall, and the archivist opened another door with a key from her ring.

If Lucy Marino's office was a stereotype of a modern workplace, then Amelia Grayson's art studio was a shrine to 19th century creativity. The space had been preserved as though the artist had simply stepped out of the room a minute ago to fetch a cup of tea. A large paint-splattered easel stood at the centre of the space, with a spindle chair placed in front. A painter's palette, with dried pools of blues ranging from aquamarine to cobalt, rested on a low table next to a jar holding several brushes. There was a large bay window, its sill littered with embroidered cushions, which Helene imagined would allow the maximum amount of natural light to enter the room.

After Helene had taken in the prosaic setting of the landscape artist, she noticed something that looked a bit incongruous in the studio. Along a far wall there was a long table holding what seemed like an antique chemistry set — the kind you might picture while reading the mysteries of Sherlock Holmes. There were test tubes and glass vessels, and even a stone mortar and matching pestle.

Spotting the focus of the journalist's attention, the archivist offered an explanation for the makeshift laboratory, "Grayson sometimes made her own paints, from flowers, vegetables, or even berries. It's how we know the newly discovered paintings are authentic. The colours have the same chemical structure of the mixtures Grayson created herself."

Helene's esteem for the late painter was starting to grow. She had walked away from a society marriage, dedicated her life to art and dabbled in chemistry. She seemed like a woman reaching for more than she had been offered in life.

"You can see why the legacy of how she lived is as important as her art," said the archivist, as if echoing Helene's thoughts. "And preserving it has become my own life's work. I don't have a husband or children, but I like to think I have contributed to a higher cause."

As a mother who was constantly picking up sticky granola wrappers and random wet towels, Helene could appreciate the appeal of tending to one room in which nothing was ever moved. A perfectly placed easel catching the light. A crochet blanket forever folded on the window seat. The room itself was picturesque enough to be the subject of a painting. But at the same time, Helene couldn't imagine anything lonelier than an art studio occupied by desiccated pots of paint.

February 12, 1886

My dearest Constance,

I have woken this morning in February to a verdant vision of a garden dappled with sunshine and dew. It is certainly one of the most pleasurable delights of residing in this harbour town, how spring arrives so early, like an overly eager visitor for tea. But I must pause to consider whether writing these joyful words is a kindness to you, knowing the grey rains of a Yorkshire spring.

On quieter days, I like to picture you in the drawing room with my niece and nephew at your feet, their small hands sketching out fierce dragons or turning the pages of an adventure novel. I know the children are the flowers of your own kind of garden, and you, my dear sister, are their sun. How I wish I could capture such a scene on canvas!

I must not spend too much of my day scribbling on paper as I have a morning appointment with my companion, Margaret. I believe I have mentioned her in previous letters. She is a schoolteacher with a great appreciation for the arts. A new acquaintance of late, I do hope to enjoy the fellowship of our friendship. We have made great plans to take a promenade through the manicured greenery of Beacon Hill Park and perhaps rest for a while under the shade of the grandest of pine trees, a muted giant of the woods. I am presently contemplating making this forest titan the subject of a new painting.

I will close this letter with a plea once more for your husband to give you leave to visit me in Canada. I know he worries about your health, but I do think taking the air of my coastal environs might be a tonic for what ails you. And more selfishly, it has been more than two and ten years since I made my journey to this new land, and I so long for your sympathetic company. Just think, if the children were to make the ocean journey with you, they would be able to write their own adventure stories! And I would adore to see their shining faces playing among the blossoms of my own humble garden. Please promise me you will think on it.

With steadfast affection,

    Amelia

Chapter 9

Sitting at her disorganized newsroom desk, with the chatter of her colleagues and the hum of the radio in the background, Helene closed the museum pamphlet containing the letters of Amelia Grayson. Despite the artist's descriptions of long walks and new friends, the separation from her sister was obviously a source of heartache. In this era of air travel and video phone calls, the journalist struggled to imagine spending a dozen years without seeing the face of a loved one. Although, to be fair, during the height of the pandemic, there was something distinctly Victorian about the prohibitions against casual encounters. It was a time when going to the grocery store held as much terror as the 20th century's first transatlantic flights.

The journalist also took a moment to give thanks that she didn't live in a time when a husband's permission was needed to visit a sister or a friend.

The obituary she had done on the life of the late curator from the Amelia Grayson Museum had gone on the radio and been posted on the web the previous evening. Helene was pleased she had managed to balance describing Marino as notable but not necessarily virtuous. There was a tendency in journalism to make dead people always sound like good people, as though dying had absolved them of their sins.

About to return to the news story she was working on, Helene's attention was caught by the opening of her producer's office door. She had been waiting for Riya to get out of a phone meeting all morning — a meeting she was sure had less to do with journalism standards and more with employee time management, as modern newsrooms were not immune to the pressures of corporate culture.

Grabbing a notebook from the pile on her desk, Helene quickly headed in the direction of the office before anyone else got there first.

"I was wondering if I could talk to you about a possible follow-up story," stated Helene, knowing the one thing her producer disliked more than a scandal without a confirmed source was a journalist who lacked confidence.

Peering over her trendy, square, white-framed glasses, Riya asked, "Aren't you supposed to be writing an update on city council's latest motion on the new swimming pool?"

"That decision doesn't come down until tomorrow. At the afternoon meeting. And what's more, both you and I know that pool is never going to get built. Half the city wants to refurbish the old one, and the other wants an Olympic-sized facility," Helene countered.

"That's exactly why it's a great story. It makes everyone in this prosaic little West Coast town furious, no matter what side they are on. And that means they can't get enough of the story. Do you know, every time we do an update, we get hundreds of angry emails? It's fabulous! Talk about audience engagement! Frankly, I couldn't be happier if the pool never gets built. The story is great for ratings, and swimming is bad for my hair. All that chlorine gets soaked in. I smell like toilet cleanser for days." At the mention of her high-maintenance curls, Riya tried to tuck a stray lock behind her ear. The rebellious tendril freed itself instantly.

"Don't worry, I'm on it," Helene reassured her producer. "And I have the phone number of the people behind the petition to stop the new pool being built on the dog park. I'll call them for comment."

This remark put a smile on Riya's face. "Dog people — they are the angriest. Like a Rottweiler with a migraine."

Most of Riya's metaphors involved health conditions plaguing the older woman.

Having placated Riya, the journalist kept going. "I was wondering about doing a second story about the curator of the Amelia Grayson Museum, the one who was murdered."

"Murdered? Have the police confirmed that?"

"No, but I have my sources." Helene didn't want to reveal that as the person who discovered the body, she was her own source. "Of course, I will wait for police confirmation, but you know how much people love Amelia Grayson. She's a Victoria icon. Any story connected with her is sure to get attention. And the short obit I wrote online got a lot of hits. Probably because the curator was one of those 'Top 40 under 40' millennials."

"I hate those people. Don't have the good manners to be young and poor like god intended. Damn overachievers. Isn't it enough that their bladders are still in good working order?"

Helene didn't think this was the moment to point out that people in their twenties and thirties faced more housing and job insecurity than any generation since the Great Depression. She had to stay on message.

"As I was saying, I was hoping to do a bit of digging into the circumstances surrounding her death as a follow-up. I've found a few red flags that need investigating. Like whether she managed to graduate from art college. Anything dodgy that might be connected to her murder."

"So, this isn't just a fluff piece? There's potential for controversy?" Her producer's eyes lit up with excitement.

"Yes," agreed Helene, not really wanting to go too far down this path. "I just need to spend some time speaking with people who went to college with her and check a few records. There is also a sister who doesn't seem particularly distraught over her death."

"All right, you can do it off the side of your desk when you finish your other stories. But I want an update on what you've learned in a couple of days. I need to know if there is going to be some meat to this story."

"You bet," replied Helene, slightly uncomfortable with the direction the conversation had gone. But at least she had bought herself some breathing room to investigate the murder a little more thoroughly.

Helene had just sat down at her desk when the phone in her pocket rang as if on cue. Reluctantly pressing the screen to answer, the journalist knew she needed to stop talking soon and get some work done.

"So, I am going to give you a bit of a heads-up," Detective Kalinowski stated brusquely, without any greeting.

"All right," responded Helene in a calm voice that belied her curiosity.

"We are sending out a press release," Kalinowski said. "But I'm giving you an hour's lead."

"What's going to be in the release?" The journalist could hardly believe the fortuitous timing of the phone call.

"Just that Marino was murdered and it was a shooting."

"What about the location of the body?" asked Helene.

"We are sharing that too," the police officer confirmed. "I imagine the breakwater will be a little busier than usual tonight. There are always freaks who want to check out the place where someone died."

Helene made a mental note to perhaps skip her evening ocean walk. Maybe she would binge on a new British TV murder mystery instead.

Kalinowski added, "I'm doing this because our investigation has stalled again. We are hoping people will call in if they have information." Helene was not surprised by this ulterior motive. Sometimes the cops needed the media to get information out to the public — a symbiotic, if not exactly trusting, relationship.

Helene decided to push her luck. "Can you tell me anything else, off the record?"

Kalinowski took a moment to consider. "This absolutely *cannot* end up on the radio, but we discovered she had been receiving anonymous hate mail. We found a stash of the letters in her office."

"Did they look like the word scrawled in the memorial book? Like they were sent by the same person?"

"Our forensic folks are still trying to determine that," replied the detective.

Helene would have loved to take a look at the written threats herself, but she knew Kalinowski was never going to let that happen.

"Thanks for giving me a chance to get it on the radio first. You'll put me in the good books with my boss."

"Well, it works both ways. I need to know if you stumble on anything significant."

"Of course," Helene said, not sure if the police knew about the fraught relationship between the curator and her sister, or the issues around the inheritance. But she wasn't going to casually send the authorities after the baker. She had gotten into journalism to protect people's rights, not to put them in prison — at least not without establishing the facts first. Helene imagined the detective had already been in touch with the sister herself, as she was the next of kin.

As Helene had expected, her producer was thrilled that the death of the curator had been confirmed as a homicide. Riya wanted copy written up for the 2:30 newscast and said the journalist could spend the rest of the day following up on leads. Helene still needed to do a quick update on the city pool the next day, but no matter how the council voted, the story wouldn't take long to put together, inserting a few quotes from the predictably outraged residents.

With renewed focus, Helene went over what she had learned so far about the curator.

Impressive career.
Unimpressive family.

Questionable ethics.

Ultimately, the journalist realized she needed to figure out exactly what had happened at art college. The archivist and Marino's sister seemed to have very different accounts of her post-secondary education, the latter believing she didn't graduate at all.

Since the Pacific Art Institute was located about an hour's drive away from Victoria, Helene knew she had to leave immediately to get back in time to make her children dinner. Thankfully, they were now old enough to walk home from school by themselves when she was too busy to pick them up. They were becoming independent, which both relieved and terrified her.

There was one more call she wanted to make, but she would wait until she was out on the open highway before connecting with her friend Alex. She packed up her notebook and a voice recorder just in case she needed it for any possible interviews, then filled up her water bottle and grabbed a granola bar from the box in her desk drawer. She never assumed there would be anything to eat or drink when she went out on a story. And hunger was the enemy of a working brain.

As she drove past the outskirts of the city, leaving behind the monotonous rows of suburban homes, the view to the right offered a grey sky over a turbulent ocean, while on the left, stretching cedar trees stood guard. Helene was grateful the rain in the forecast seemed to be holding off.

After a few minutes of enjoying the rhythm of the road and the beauty of the passing landscape, Helene called up her friend on the car's Bluetooth.

Alex picked up on the first ring, maintaining the eagerness of a cub reporter after fifteen years on the job.

"Hey, it's me," stated Helene. "I know you're probably busy, but I wanted to flag that the cops are sending out a press release soon. It confirms the murder of Marino."

"And how do you know this?" asked Alex with justifiable suspicion.

"I have my sources," said Helene. "However," she continued, changing the subject, "I am also hoping you can use your unsung talents to help get hold of a document for me — a will, to be specific."

"The will of the curator?"

"Actually, her mother's."

"Is she also dead?"

"Yes," affirmed Helene.

"Okay, good. That will make it much easier," Alex responded with typical newsroom insensitivity. "What exactly am I looking for?"

"What is anyone ever looking for in a will? Who got the goods and who didn't. And how much any house or estate might be worth. What I've been told is that Marino may have cheated her sister out of an inheritance."

"You think she was murdered by her sister?" Alex was intrigued.

"Let's just say there wasn't a lot of love lost between them."

Helene then shared the correct spelling of Marino's mother's name, along with her dates of birth and death. She had asked for her friend's help because she absolutely despised sifting through legal documents, her eyes glazing over points and sub-points. Alex, on the other hand, viewed papers like court filings as a puzzle that needed solving. And she had broken many important and exciting stories after spending countless hours combing through boxes of dusty records, teasing out their secrets with the patience of a seasoned hunter.

Helene had been about to hang up when Alex spoke again. "Do you mind if I ask your advice?"

The journalist was taken aback. Her friend was not the type to seek guidance, usually unapologetically taking what she wanted from life.

"Sure, what's on your mind?"

"Should I get a cat?"

Helene had to stop herself from bursting into laughter. Alex had no children and no partner. She had never indicated any desire to share her home with another living creature.

"Well, I may not be the best person to ask," replied Helene cautiously, not wanting to dissuade her friend. "I already have two creatures to clean up after. And why a cat? What about a dog?"

"Those emotionally dependent excuses for canines? I'd rather have a wolf." This sounded more like typical Alex. "Dogs are just too sloppy with affection. It's embarrassing."

"You know what? I think a cat sounds perfect for you," encouraged Helene. "Just make sure you put a bell on its neck, so it doesn't eat all the songbirds."

"A bell on its neck? How undignified. It's not a goddamn reindeer pulling a sleigh."

After an affectionate chuckle and a quick goodbye, Helene continued her drive along the strip of wild highway, secure in the knowledge that a loyal and fierce feline would always live in the untamed heart of her friend.

Chapter 10

Walking through the halls of the Visual Arts Building at the Pacific Art Institute, Helene took in the familiar scents and sounds of academia and creativity. It was a mixture of paint fumes, old coffee, furiously scanning copy machines and the laughter of those who believed their youth would last forever. The halls of the mid-century building were hung with the works of students past and present, as the dates on the tiny cards holding the names of the artists indicated. The creations ranged from a multimedia composition weaving together old telephone cords and what appeared to be real human hair to a more classical portrait of a poodle, albeit wearing sunglasses. Helene wondered what Amelia Grayson would make of the modern pieces. The painter had experimented with her own style of impressionism, considered avant-garde at the time, but maybe these pieces were too ungoverned to have been appreciated by the Victorian artist.

Helene was very familiar with the world of higher education as her childhood home had been a few blocks away from the University of Alberta in Edmonton. Both of her parents had been academics — her father, a scientist who decoded DNA in the hopes of curing cancer, her mother, a professor of music with a collection of medieval recorders stashed in the hall closet. When she was young, most of Helene's free time was spent on campus, going swimming with friends at the university pool or dining at the exclusive faculty club, which served a baked Alaska dessert. The mystery of the frozen ice cream inside the cooked meringue was a constant source of delight and consternation, like one of the tricks her father performed for children in his laboratory, featuring dry ice.

After climbing two sets of stairs, Helene arrived in a hallway of professors' offices, knocking on the first door with confidence. The journalist was not easily intimidated by academics who were used to commanding a lecture hall of undergraduates. She had seen too many drunk tenured intellectuals stumbling out the front door after one of her parents' famous dinner parties to take them seriously.

It took a second round of thumping against the door with a plaque that read PROFESSOR WHYTE before the handle turned from the inside.

"What is it?" A woman who appeared to be in her mid-thirties, with a pair of glasses perched on her head, opened the door only enough to peek at the visitor.

"I'm Helene from Vancouver Island Radio, and I was hoping you could help me with a story I'm working on." The journalist knew that the ego of an academic could rarely resist a request for research assistance. "It's to do with the background of one of the students. What her time was like at the Institute."

Professor Whyte looked Helene over one more time and then opened the door, allowing her to enter. The journalist followed the woman into a room littered with brightly painted canvases and thick textbooks, about what she would expect from the den of an art professor.

Although the academic appeared to be at least ten years younger than Helene, her style of dress was firmly entrenched in the 1960s. She wore a long, shapeless kaftan tie-dyed in orange and brilliant yellow. On her feet she sported leather sandals with thick purple knitted socks. Her hair hung in two braids more suited to a schoolgirl than an academic, but Helene imagined what the professor lost in style was made up for in comfort. She envied the woman's complete disregard for the dictates of 21st century fashion.

"What's this about?" Professor Whyte asked after settling herself in the padded chair behind the desk, motioning for Helene to take the seat opposite. The wooden offering, which looked much less comfortable, was currently covered in a stack of books which the journalist moved to a nearby window ledge before sitting down.

"Well, I know it's a long shot, but I'm trying to find out more about Lucy Marino. I'm not sure if you've heard, but she was murdered recently."

Professor Whyte's face took on a stunned expression. "I knew she had died, but not murdered. That's awful."

"Yes, the police have just confirmed it," said Helene, but then moved on quickly. "I was hoping to learn about her time here as a student. I've been told she was tremendously gifted but also may have run into some trouble." The journalist didn't want to lead the woman too much, but still thought it necessary to hint that she already knew there might have been some sort of scandal.

"I had no idea the mainstream media was so interested in the world of art," stated Professor Whyte.

"To be honest, without the murder, we probably wouldn't be."

Whyte smiled in response. "Well, to be fair, nothing is better for the career of an artist than their untimely death. The value of their work shoots up immediately."

Shifting her gaze to the window and the view of a campus quadrant below, the professor appeared to be debating whether to disclose what she knew to Helene. It didn't take long for her to reach a decision. "As it happens, Lucy was a few years behind me in college. We were never in the same class, but I certainly heard enough about her."

"I understand she was very talented."

"She was. Absolutely. And at the start she was very much the new darling of the department. She could do any style with any medium. Realistic, pointillism, the pop art of Andy Warhol, the skies of Vermeer. As a student in my final

71

year, I was more than a little resentful of the attention she received. Especially when she seemed to create compositions with such ease. For me, painting has always been a painstaking process."

The academic paused again, as though replaying her own days as a student in her mind. Helene waited patiently for the story to continue.

"But then something happened. It soon became apparent that she could recreate every technique of art since the smile of the Mona Lisa was first put to canvas, but she did not have a style of her own. Everything she did was derivative. She was a master imitator without a vision. A performing monkey, to use a phrase that is deeply problematic."

"What happened?"

"Well, I don't want to find myself quoted on what I say next. It is all second-hand, as I was three years ahead of her, but things appeared to go badly. She fell out of favour with some of the faculty."

"Do you know if she actually graduated?"

"As far as I can remember, no. I think she stuck it out for the second term and then simply disappeared. A few years later I heard she was the curator at the Grayson Museum. That came as a bit of a shock, but I assumed she had completed her education elsewhere."

"Is there someone on staff who may have taught Marino?"

Professor Whyte cocked her head to one side thoughtfully. "Funny you should ask. I believe Professor Neumann has office hours today. And this is very, very third hand, but it is rumoured he had an affair with Marino."

"That still happens?" asked Helene.

"Not so much anymore. A lot has changed in the past few years of the Me Too movement. But this is more than a decade ago." Professor Whyte shared a mischievous smile. "Do you want me to ask him to come to my office?"

Helene only needed a few seconds to decide. "Sure. But what reason will you give?"

"I'll offer him some of my famous gingersnap cookies. He can't resist them. I happened to bake a batch last night." Whyte picked up the handset of the office phone but paused before dialling. "A word of warning. If you want to stay on his good side, try not to make him feel 'cancelled.' There is nothing quite so fragile as the ego of a tenured professor who can no longer get his first-year students into bed."

After Professor Whyte had made the call to her colleague down the hall, it was only a short wait until there was an energetic rap on the door followed by a cheery hello.

Professor Neumann entered the room and immediately zeroed in on the tin of homemade gingersnap cookies on the desk. However, he stopped short when he spotted Helene in the wooden chair.

"I didn't know you had a visitor." The professor turned toward Helene with what she imagined was supposed to be a charming smile. He was wearing an argyle sweater vest which matched his pompous British accent. Possessing a head of salt-and-pepper hair and strong chin, he had the looks to take advantage of impressionable students. He extended an elegant hand in greeting.

"Professor Neumann. A pleasure, to be sure."

"Helene Unger, Vancouver Island Radio." Despite the warning from Whyte to go gently, the journalist decided to dive right in. "I'm doing a piece on Lucy Marino. The Amelia Grayson curator who died."

Professor Neumann retrieved his proffered hand. "That bloody trollop? Good riddance to her."

Helene abruptly shifted back in her chair as though she had been slapped by his words. But not wishing to give the academic the satisfaction of thinking he had made her uncomfortable, the journalist continued. "I was just wondering if you wanted to make any comment about her time here as a student. I think you taught her."

73

"I have absolutely nothing to say. And, in fact, I am overdue for a lecture." The academic reached forward and grabbed two cookies from the tin, clearly believing he had earned them. He then strode out of the room with his chest puffed out like an indignant peacock.

"As you can see, he has some of that Old World charm," stated Professor Whyte after he left the room. "Retirement can't come soon enough."

Helene almost added that she was all too familiar with the likes of Professor Neumann as similar characters had populated the childhood she'd spent on a university campus. Instead, she said, "Well, I certainly seemed to have hit a nerve. I wonder if any of her classmates would be more open to talking."

"I could probably track down a list of those who were in the same year as her. Why don't you leave me your email?"

"I'd really appreciate that," replied Helene, wondering if the academic's eagerness to assist was in part fuelled by a desire to spite her arrogant colleague. She couldn't blame her.

Thanking Professor Whyte for sharing her time and candid comments, Helene also helped herself to a gingersnap cookie as they looked much more appealing than the crushed granola bar in her backpack.

Thoughts of where to find a proper, if late, lunch on campus before the return drive to Victoria flitted through her mind as she walked back down the hallway. However, when she spied that the door of Professor Neumann's office was slightly ajar, she decided food could wait.

Helene didn't strictly consider herself an investigative journalist, and entering someone's office without permission wasn't something she did casually. But the antipathy the academic had expressed toward Lucy Marino made her think he was hiding something. And she figured she owed it to all the young female students of whom he had taken advantage to see if she could uncover his secrets.

Cautiously pushing the door open and calling out a hello, Helene was relieved to discover an empty room. It was a space that was fastidiously organized, especially relative to the creative chaos of Professor Whyte's domain. The spines of the books on the shelves were all lined up neatly and the desk was miraculously free of stray papers. There were several lush ferns in the corner, reminiscent of foliage suited to a 19th century English drawing room. The paintings on the walls were landscapes, one depicting the gentle rolling hills of a countryside, the other, a Venetian canal. It all seemed a bit traditional for someone who was meant to encourage students to discover their own voice.

Uncomfortably cognizant that she was trespassing, Helene headed for a filing cabinet in the corner, but a quick shuffle through papers revealed nothing more than course outlines for painting classes. Her armpits growing sticky with nervous sweat, Helene decided to swiftly inspect the contents of the desk and then make her getaway. As she moved behind the substantial piece of furniture, she pushed away thoughts of having to explain her actions to Detective Kalinowski.

Several bottles of Scotch clanked against each other when Helene pulled open the first drawer, but nothing else of interest was inside. Moving on to the second drawer, Helene discovered several key rings and a folder marked PRIVATE. Feeling a whisper of excitement, the journalist retrieved the file from the drawer and laid it open on the tidy desk. That's when she knew her bad behaviour had borne fruit.

In the same thick red ink that had been scrawled across the memorial book at Lucy Marino's service was a note that read, YOU RUINED MY LIFE, AND YOU WILL PAY! There were several other papers underneath, all containing similar vicious messages. Taking out her phone, she rapidly took pictures of the threats, then returned the folder to the drawer and fled from the office.

Safely behind the wheel of her car, a plastic container of sushi on the seat next to her from the student cafeteria, Helene could only wonder what exactly had unfolded during Marino's time at the art college. Whatever it was, it must have left a substantial legacy of hate for Professor Neumann to send nasty letters to the curator so many years later — not to mention secretly slipping into the museum service to desecrate the memorial book. The journalist also had to consider whether this hate had ultimately led to murder.

Chapter 11

Running her fingers over the dresses and sweaters hanging in her crowded closet, Helene was impressed by the numerous shades of grey she owned, her collection of clothing was like a rainbow that had been bled of its colour. She couldn't remember an exact moment in her life when she decided to adopt such a monochrome uniform, but it was probably after giving birth to her second child and realizing her brain no longer had the resources to coordinate a colourful wardrobe. There were a few exceptions to the rule, like a bright pink acrylic sweater hanging at the end of the rack — a much-cherished garment that rarely saw the light of day. And when picking her outfit for that evening, she predictably selected a grey top with dark checked pants. In a nod to the formality of the occasion, she would once again swap out her backpack for a large purse.

Earlier that day, Helene had been surprised to receive an email from the Grayson Museum archivist, inviting her to a special preview of the newly discovered paintings. The artwork wouldn't be shared with the general public for a couple more weeks, but a few members of the media, including herself, were invited for a sneak peek that evening. They just had to agree to keep the story embargoed until the wider unveiling.

In a moment of cynicism, the journalist couldn't help but wonder if the staff were trying to capitalize on the interest in the murder of their curator to bring more attention to Grayson's art. It seemed like Marino was still working for the museum, even from the grave.

It had been a long time since Helene had dressed up to go out in the evening, having abandoned all attempts at dating a few years ago. After several relationships had sputtered out in a matter of months, Helene realized that, for the first time in her life, she preferred being single. Her work satisfied her intellectual needs, and her children fulfilled the emotional ones. She knew this might change one day, but right now she revelled in the fact that she no longer craved any kind of romance. It was like being freed from an addiction most women never questioned.

She did, however, have someone to accompany her at the art unveiling. Her friend Alex had also received an invitation and was going to meet her at the museum. Helene was curious as to whether the print journalist had managed to track down the will of Marino's mother, so they could confirm if the inheritance of a house was a possible motive for murder.

The journalist had cooked separate allergy-safe dinners for her two children, made sure they knew where their epinephrine kits were located and gave them permission to watch shows on their tablets until she returned home. In her son's case, "shows" meant video games containing almost as much death as a national radio broadcast.

Helene had planned to walk to the museum, which was located just a few blocks away from her home. However, there was an intense storm blowing off the ocean that evening, the kind against which an umbrella stood no chance as the rain seemed to be pouring both vertically and horizontally. Slipping behind the wheel of her car, she was grateful for the protection from the elements. The sound of the rain beating down on the metal roof reminded her of taking shelter in a log cabin during a prairie hailstorm as a child. Nothing made the indoors more welcoming than an unwelcoming outdoors.

By the time she had managed the slow drive along the narrow dark streets and the fast dash from the car to the museum's front door, Helene was wondering whether leaving the house was a mistake. The front of her pants was soaking and her hair was starting to kink in the humidity. Still, she knew it was necessary and maybe even healthy to force herself to go out after work, as she rarely made plans beyond her regular breakwater exercise. And, of course, the whipping wind and crashing waves had made her visit to the ocean all but unsafe that evening.

Feeling a bit grumpy and grey, from the rain as much as her dull pants and sweater, Helene was shocked when Alex walked into the main hall in an outfit that defied the miserable weather. She was wearing a cherry-red velvet dress which was short enough to show off her athletic legs. A set of pearls in the style of Jackie Kennedy adorned her neck, matching the style of the 1950s clutch she was carrying. Only the heavy black boots on her feet assured Helene that her friend had not been kidnapped, or at least dressed, by aliens. Since the first time they had bumped into each other at a press conference more than a decade ago, Alex had always cultivated the appearance of a disaffected university student, usually sporting her worn grey trench coat. Helene could only assume her friend was going through a life transition as she had recently expressed the desire to adopt a pet as well as to dress like a diva from a Hitchcock film. Helene decided she needed to take her friend out for a drink and find out what was going on.

"Nice outfit." Helene could not let her friend's grand entrance pass without comment. In a room full of women wearing clothes geared toward comfort and warmth rather than style, Alex stood out like an orchid among carnations.

"Thanks. I thought it might be fun to cause a bit of a stir."

Helene felt relieved as Alex at least sounded decidedly like herself.

"Is there anything to drink this time?" asked Alex, looking around the museum gallery hopefully.

"There is some tea," offered Helene with an uninspired shrug.

"Tea doesn't count, darling, and you know that."

Helene had to agree that nothing short of a martini glass would complement her friend's remarkable outfit. Alex, however, had come prepared, pulling a small flask from her vinyl purse.

"Bottoms up," she said before taking a swig and passing the flask to Helene. Indulging in the smallest of sips, as she was driving that night, Helene did appreciate the warmth of the aged whisky as it flowed through her chilled body.

They didn't have to wait much longer before the woman who had led the memorial service for Lucy Marino ascended the stage once more, forgoing the malfunctioning microphone on this occasion. On either side of her stood two easels covered with black cloths, hiding the paintings underneath from view.

"I want to thank everyone who came out on this wet evening in March to celebrate these newly discovered works of Amelia Grayson. We are sure it will be worth your while. But before we begin, we want to dedicate this event to Lucy Marino, our late curator who so recently and tragically lost her life. She was responsible for discovering and confirming the authenticity of these paintings."

The museum director then paused as though offering a moment of silence for the departed.

"I also want to thank the anonymous individual who donated these paintings to the museum. They would accept no compensation, simply wanting to enrich the legacy of Grayson's work."

The director, who Helene recalled was named Ivy, then walked over to stand in the middle of the pair of paintings. She grasped one corner of the two covering cloths in each of her hands.

80

"So, without further ado, I offer you these breathtaking works of Amelia Grayson, one of the most remarkable artists to ever call Victoria her home."

With a flap of the cloths being removed, the two landscapes were revealed to the room. The crowd took several steps forward in unison, everyone trying to get a better look at the works. On the left, a painting depicted a stand of Douglas Fir trees, the kind that had grown for hundreds of years in Beacon Hill Park. The subject and brushwork were definitely in the style of Amelia Grayson.

On initial glance, the second painting also seemed to be typical of the artist — a beach scene, waves, and clouds formed with whirling impressionist strokes. And yet, when Helene examined the piece more carefully, she saw that there was a figure labouring at the edge of the water, the net in his hands marking him as a fisherman. Although Grayson admittedly was commissioned for portraiture work, as far as Helene knew the artist never included humans in her landscapes. And from the growing buzz in the room, Helene knew she was not the only one who was surprised by the new direction taken by the painter. Even more curiously, there seemed to be something familiar about the figure painted into the scene. But Helene's brain refused to make the connection.

"What's wrong?" asked Alex, her instinct as a journalist sharp as ever.

"Nothing's wrong, per se," said Helene. "Just peculiar. Grayson doesn't usually include people in her landscape paintings."

"Does this mean they could be fakes?" inquired her friend, smelling a possible scandal.

"Apparently, they were authenticated. Perhaps Grayson was just exploring a new style."

"Oh," responded Alex, making no effort to hide her disappointment. "They aren't going to hold the presses for this story." Taking another surreptitious sip from her flask,

Alex stated, "I do, on the other hand, have some news that actually might be considered interesting, I tracked down the will."

Helene pulled her concentration away from the two paintings, took hold of her friend's elbow, and steered the two of them to a quieter part of the room.

"What did you find out?"

"Well, I don't have siblings, but I can only imagine that if one sister inherited a mansion in Moss Bay while the other received nothing, it would create a bit of tension."

"Lucy got everything?" asked Helene with growing excitement.

"To be fair, Paola got the mother's drinks cabinet. It seems Lucy didn't imbibe."

"Was it a nice drinks cabinet?"

Alex looked at her friend with incredulity. "I don't think there is a gin strong enough to take the sting out of not getting half of a mansion in Moss Bay. With today's prices, it is probably worth close to three million."

"I guess the sister really did have a reason to hate Lucy. That said, she did tell me about the inheritance herself. She wasn't trying to hide it."

"But did she tell you about the codicil in the will?" Alex's eyes were lit up like a magician about to perform their final trick.

"What codicil?"

"If Lucy died within five years of inheriting the house, it all went to the sister. Giving Paola a very nice place to park her drinks cabinet."

Helene felt her heart race at learning this new information. "And when did Lucy inherit the house?"

"Just over four and half years ago. So, time was running out."

The codicil to the will certainly made the timing of Lucy's death suspicious. And, recalling her meeting with the sister a few days earlier, Helene knew the bakery was in

82

desperate need of an injection of cash. If Paola Marino sold her mother's house in Moss Bay, she wouldn't have to worry about demanding customers or malfunctioning ovens ever again. It was the kind of freedom that some people might just kill for.

February 25, 1886

My dearest Constance,

    As you are unable to make the ocean voyage to the country I now call home, I am instead sending you a watercolour of its bucolic splendour. Spending so much of my time out of doors, I do now believe that if there is a god, he or she is to be found in nature. Is there not perfection in the symmetry of a simple blossom or the fragrance of rain at dawn? As you know, the dusty nave of a crumbling church and the weathered hymnals clutched by joyless matrons have never held much allure for me. I do find sympathy for my predilection to embrace the wisdom of nature in the words of William Wordsworth:

> *One impulse from a vernal wood*
> *May teach you more of man,*
> *Of moral evil and of good,*
> *Than all the sages can.*

    And as I have in recent weeks come to especially savour the solace that the natural world has to offer, I conversely do find the company of some others almost tiresome. My friend Margaret, of whom I was growing most fond, endeavours to spend every afternoon by my side. I think she may not, like so many, understand that an artist craves time to themselves in order to hear the elusive call of inspiration. I have had to become very creative in my litany of excuses to put her off, and the half-truths do weigh heavy upon my soul. At times, I even find it necessary to sneak a dollop of gin into my teacup to sustain interest in our conversations. This disharmony has affirmed my avoidance of the state of matrimony. One so partial to their own company can hardly possess the qualities of a good wife and mother.

The only companionship for which I do indeed have an unceasing desire is yours, my dear sister. But I will not write at length on this theme again, as my pleading has become tedious even to my own self.

Please send news of my niece and nephew, of whom I do think often. And also word of your health. I am convinced you do not spend enough time convalescing after a serious episode. I am hopeful the new physician you mentioned in your last letter has some restorative remedies to suggest.

With steadfast affection,

Amelia

Chapter 12

In theory, Helene could appreciate flowers as much as Amelia Grayson — the shapely petals, the deep vibrant colours, the short life cycle which made them even more precious. However, in reality, if flowers were brought into her home she was often irritated by the strong smells and ultimately the sneezes they elicited from her children. She considered flowers to be a bit like loud people who dominated a room without consideration for others. And like loud people, they were generally to be avoided, except if a close encounter helped to uncover the truth. That is why she entered Benjamin's Flower Shop on a Friday morning with a sense of anticipation and reluctance.

The name Benjamin Cornish was included on a list of former classmates of Lucy Marino during her time at the Pacific Art Institute. Professor Whyte had texted her the information, with an asterisk next to names of people she thought had been close to the late curator when she was a student. Before arriving at the flower shop, Helene had in fact started by looking up a woman named Rosa Winter, as her name was the first to be highlighted on the list.

When the journalist did an online search for Winter, it appeared she was making a living as an artist, the first person she had encountered with a connection to the Art Institute who was doing so. Helene had been wondering if the place only turned out professors and curators.

Winter painted cheerful street scenes of popular places like Cook Street Village and Fisherman's Wharf. The artist used bright pigments in a style that was somewhere on the continuum between a cartoon and a happy sort of surrealism of curving roads and slouching trees. Helene imagined this kind of art was a hit with tourists who liked to see Victoria in an idealized state, not as a modern city struggling to cope with homelessness and the opioid crisis.

While she was sifting through the artist's online gallery, Helene came across a painting Winter had done of the Moss Bay Marina. The work was more in the tradition of impressionism, depicting the vivid swirls of the currents against the horizontal grain of the wooden docks. Winter had used a different colour for the paintwork of each boat, and the vessels all listed at slight angles, conveying the rocking motion of the water. Despite the fact that Helene avoided boats as a rule, this painting still held great appeal for her. It communicated the restless spirit of coastal living.

"I remember Lucy well," said Winter, after Helene had introduced herself over the phone. "She was not a very happy person, even when she was happy. Manic, if you know what I mean." Winter was the kind of individual who was comfortable having conversations about emotional wellbeing.

"Were you close to her?" asked Helene.

"At first, I thought we would become good friends. She was very intense about painting in a way I'd never encountered before. I was from a small town and had always felt like a bit of an oddball for being into art. But I quickly figured out that Lucy was a human roller coaster, so I kept my distance after that."

"What about your other classmates?"

"Oh, some people are attracted to that kind of energy. And she had a small crowd she hung out with. But they seemed more like followers than friends. Devotees, almost."

Marino went over the list of other students on the phone with Winter, who confirmed a couple of names she thought belonged to Marino's crowd for the first year of art college. But the painter had no idea what had happened to them since graduation. As far as she knew, they weren't working as artists in Victoria, she would have run into them at a show or opening.

The next person Helene tracked down through an online search was Benjamin Cornish, who since leaving art school had apparently gone on to build a chain of local flower shops. Helene presumed his own dreams of becoming a painter had not panned out. But if he had failed in the realm of creativity, he had succeeded in the world of commerce, evidenced by his ownership of almost half a dozen shops in Greater Victoria.

By calling ahead to one of the flower shops, she found out that Cornish usually worked out of the Fernwood location on Friday mornings, so she planned an impromptu visit. And that's how she found herself considering neon blue tulips on a grey morning in March.

"May I help you?" A tall man had come around from behind the counter to stand next to Helene. He had brushed a lock of blond hair out of his eyes while speaking.

"I assume those aren't natural," asked Helene, pointing at the glowing tulips.

"They are *enhanced*, sweetheart. But aren't we all?" the man replied with a touch of brashness.

Helene smiled in response. It was refreshing to meet someone who gave off a bit of flavour in a town where most people wouldn't meet your eyes when passing along the sidewalk — a coldness residents had inherited from the British colonizers.

After her unfruitful interaction with Professor Neumann, the journalist decided to take an indirect approach to getting information out of Cornish.

"I need something to send to a friend who lost her sister," she explained. The idea occurred to the journalist in the same moment she said it out loud.

Cornish responded with unguarded compassion. "I am so sorry. I hope she wasn't terribly young." The florist was obviously used to working with the recently bereaved.

"In her early thirties, in fact. It's quite tragic. And the police are even investigating."

Cornish seemed to go a few shades paler in reaction to this news, like a flower slipping under the shade of a cloud. "That is simply awful," he stated, and then quickly recovered. "Why don't we take a look at some orchids? Always so elegant yet understated."

A few minutes later, Helene found herself paying for an oversized bouquet, the arrangement of the graceful white blossoms making it evident that Cornish was a sort of artist.

"And what is the sister's name and address for delivery?"

"It's Paola Marino, the sister of Lucy Marino. She was a curator of a local art museum. Perhaps you've heard of her?"

Helene watched as shifting emotions subtly played out across the face of the florist. The drip of a tap behind the counter seemed oppressively loud while the journalist waited for a response.

"Lucy Marino?" he finally stated without meeting Helene's eyes. "No, that name isn't familiar." It was the most unconvincing lie Helene had heard since her son had denied eating a bag of dairy-free chocolate chips while still chewing on the sweet remains.

"Right, well, I am very grateful for you putting this together quickly. It means so much to make a small gesture for someone who is grieving." As she spoke, Helene recalled the callous tones used by Paola when speaking about the death of her sister. But there had to be some sort of grief buried under all that sibling resentment.

"I am only happy to be able to help in difficult times." Despite the sympathetic words he spoke, Benjamin had not recovered his composure since the mention of Lucy Marino.

"Is it a sort of art, the flower arranging?" Helene said, seeing if she could unsettle the florist even further.

"Art? Oh no. Art can be cruel and sometimes even ugly. Whereas flowers are always a kindness, a gift of love or a panacea to the isolation of grief." Benjamin had spoken

89

the words passionately. Realizing he had perhaps revealed too much, he got back to the business at hand. "Now, let me get the rest of that address from you. I have other pressing orders to prepare."

Helene decided to send the flowers to the bakery as she didn't have a home address for Marino's sister. She was curious as to how the woman would react to the floral gift, somehow doubting it would be perceived as a kindness.

After completing the order, Benjamin could only have gotten rid of Helene more quickly if he had physically pushed her out the front door. The business owner was so flustered he had forgotten to ask about a message for the sympathy card. This suited the journalist just fine as she wanted to keep it anonymous. It was a pity, however, that newsroom budgets didn't stretch to bouquets for people you thought might have committed murder. Orchids were stunning but costly.

Following her visit to the flower shop, Helene returned to the newsroom and put together an overdue story about the city council decision on the new pool. They had unanimously voted to hold a referendum on the facility, which was just an expensive way of delaying a decision. This non-binding public vote had the added bonus of appearing to be a type of community engagement.

Later that afternoon, when the pressure to meet deadlines had passed, Helene had time to reflect on her encounter at the flower shop. She couldn't imagine why Benjamin Cornish would lie about going to art college with Marino unless he had something to hide. And if someone who had a guilty conscience hid the truth, then did that mean Professor Neumann's open hatred of the curator in fact proved his innocence? But what about the angry and bitter notes she had found in his desk drawer — why would he bother sending them to Marino so many years after she had left the Institute? But Paola Marino had also made no effort to hide her antipathy toward her sister. Maybe the next thing she needed to do was track down the house in Moss Bay, which was at the heart of the coveted inheritance. But first she wanted to arrange another visit to the museum.

After her radio producer had learned of Helene's attendance at the exclusive viewing of the newly discovered paintings by Amelia Grayson, her interest in the story had heightened. Riya now wanted Helene to do a short radio documentary on Grayson that would go live the day the works were shared with the public. Of course, the mystery of the curator's murder also needed to be part of the piece. In addition, Riya asked the journalist to write up a matching story to go on the web with high-quality photos of the paintings themselves. Helene had decided there were a few other shots she needed to include in her story.

"Hello Hana, it's Helene from Vancouver Island Radio." The journalist was glad she recalled the first name of the archivist from their earlier encounter. Remembering and using names was a trick of the trade to make people more willing to help you. "First of all, I want to thank you for inviting me to the preview. It was an incredible honour."

"Of course," replied the archivist. "Anything that will help bring more attention to Grayson's legacy."

Not one to miss an opening, Helene dived in. "Speaking of which, we are thinking of doing a special feature on the new paintings, looking at the life of the painter as well."

"Oh my!" responded the archivist. From the delight in her tone, Helene suspected she would get little resistance to her plan.

"I was hoping to take some photos of the house — I mean, the museum — to add to the piece. The other day when I was visiting, I was especially intrigued by her studio. And her makeshift laboratory, where she created her paints. I think it would be very interesting to our listeners."

"That all sounds very good. I will just need to run your visit by our executive director, Ivy, and I'll get back to you. We could plan for some time early next week if that works?"

"Great, and thanks again, Hana." She was a little surprised the archivist needed to check with her boss, but maybe the staff were taking extra precautions since the murder.

As it was Friday, Helene decided to pack up her things a little early and get home to her kids. She felt like the murder investigation had been taking priority, and she was determined to give them some undivided attention. She would suggest watching one of their favourite movies together tucked up in her king-sized bed. It was a cozy family tradition even her teenage daughter couldn't resist.

Chapter 13

The Friday evening she spent laughing with her children helped Helene refocus her thoughts. She realized she had been devoting too much mental energy trying to figure out who had murdered Lucy Marino. It was like a puzzle that tugged at her brain, continually laying out different scenarios and suspects. She was drawn to the challenge of a mystery, but it could also distract her from paying attention to the more mundane but necessary responsibilities in life.

What's for breakfast?
Is there more toothpaste?
Have you seen my other shoe?

Debating the motives for murder had to give way to the demands for crispy bacon and soft socks.

Helene also took extra pleasure in visiting the breakwater on Saturday. After a couple of days of warmer temperatures, a cool breeze had returned, resulting in fewer walkers to avoid when aiming her lens. That morning, she managed to take a picture that made it appear as if the sun was resting on the end of the breakwater path, radiating beams and shadows in the bright early light. While she was manipulating her camera, balancing the composition of ocean and land, trying to catch the pink in the clouds, she didn't notice her fingers growing numb with cold. It reminded her of when she did ballet as a teenager and she only felt the pain of her bleeding toes after leaving the stage.

Although there were fewer people on the breakwater that morning, Helene was not entirely alone. There was a small crowd of open-water swimming enthusiasts on the beach, peeling off terrycloth jackets typically worn by Olympic athletes. They only stayed in the ocean for a couple of minutes before racing back to the shore for warm clothing.

Helene had once interviewed a swimmer for a radio story, and they had claimed the daily glacial ritual resulted in a sort of body euphoria that lasted for hours. Although Helene was in no rush to adopt their practice, having experienced enough cold for a lifetime during her Alberta childhood, she felt that the swimmers' communion with the ocean was not dissimilar to the siren call of her daily breakwater promenade.

Two days later, after a weekend of taking long walks by herself and doing complicated puzzles with her children, Helene arrived back at the office feeling rejuvenated, determined to apply herself to new stories. In the last week she had trespassed in a professor's office, ordered unnecessary and expensive orchids and wasted an afternoon touring the museum of a 19th century artist. With little to show for her efforts, Helene decided maybe it was time to let the police do their job while she got back to journalism.

Once she had surveyed the weekend newspapers, Helene searched through emails from listeners in the hopes someone had sent the station an interesting story that merited further investigation. Unfortunately, this meant reading through urgent messages warning of pharmaceutical conspiracies and alien sightings, a symptom of the modern epidemic of loneliness. She had just deleted an email about how electric cars were causing cancer when she received a text from Alex, who was at the station's front door.

Helene buzzed her friend into the building, met her at the elevator and then took her to the kitchen for a cup of tea. Before sitting down, Alex passed Helene a box of chocolates with her name on it.

"You shouldn't have . . .?" Helene asked with confusion. Spontaneous gifts were not something that had featured in their friendship before.

"I didn't," laughed Alex. "They were just at the reception desk, so they asked me to bring them upstairs to you."

"Thanks. I can't imagine who sent them," said Helene while eying up the box. "Maybe a publishing house because I put one of their authors on the radio. But you'd think there would be a note. Must have fallen off."

"Well, as they say, don't look a gift horse in the mouth, especially when the horse is a bunch of chocolates." Alex slipped off the lid of the box and inspected the contents with a concentration usually reserved for city council agendas.

Helene pulled out the information sheet that identified the different kinds of chocolates. After a moment of reading, she stated, "These all have nuts in them, so I better not. I don't want to get anything on me that I might take home to my kids."

"Right, allergies," said Helene. "Well then, I shall relieve you of your burden." With that statement, she popped one of the dainty treats into her mouth.

"Not bad. Dark chocolate, a hint of caramel and cashews."

"Well, I am glad you are enjoying my gift, and of course I'm always happy to see you, but what exactly are you doing here?" Helene asked with curiosity.

Alex finished chewing and then stated, "It appears I've decided to take the plunge."

"Take the plunge?" A vision of her friend walking down the aisle in a long white dress and big black boots flashed through Helene's mind, but she instantly dismissed it as entirely improbable.

"I'm picking up a cat this morning — well, a kitten. From a local shelter."

"That's fabulous," said Helene with a sense of relief, although she understood that, for her friend, this level of commitment was equivalent to other people getting engaged.

"And I was just wondering — if you don't think it's too much to ask — if you would consider being the cat's godparent," Alex asked hopefully. "You know, in case anything happens to me."

Helene wasn't sure how to respond. She didn't realize securing a guardian for a pet was something people did these days. Actually, she was pretty sure it wasn't. But she didn't want to say anything to dampen her friend's enthusiasm.

"I suppose that's okay. I mean, I'm only allergic to dogs. But do you really think it's necessary?"

"I just want to make sure my fur baby will be taken care of. It's the responsible thing to do."

Helene was impressed that her friend seemed to be taking the acquisition of a cat quite seriously. Maybe too seriously?

"Can I just ask," Helene probed as gently as possible, "What brought on this urge for pet ownership?"

"First of all, I don't like to think of it like that. I don't believe one creature can 'own' another. But," she continued, "since you asked, I guess I feel like I have spent *my* life writing about other people living *their* lives, you know, following *their* dreams. Cycling across the country, publishing books, even running for city council. For once I want to be the person in the story, not the one writing it."

"And that means getting a cat?"

"It's a start," replied Alex, slightly defensively. "I mean, I'm not going to have kids. I have never wanted that. But I think I need to have something or someone that isn't connected to my job. All I've done since graduation is be a journalist. I want to have some kind of identity that's separate from work, that's my own."

In response, Helene leaned over and gave her friend a hug. It wasn't the most natural of moments since they never had been huggers. But maybe this was a day for new beginnings, Helene told herself.

"Well, what are you waiting for?" asked Helene after pulling back from the awkward embrace. "Go get yourself a cat!"

Waiting at the elevator to say goodbye to her friend, Helene let out a chuckle. "I bet you haven't even considered how this is going to blow up your social media feed. Think about it, cat photos? Or, even better, kitten videos?"

"You're right, this could be bigger than members of the Royal Family wearing ugly hats!" jested Alex.

"And much cuter."

When the elevator arrived, Alex stepped in and turned around.

"By the way, what's going on with the murder investigation?"

Helene shrugged and replied, "I'm just taking a bit of a break from it."

"A bit of a break? That doesn't sound like you."

"Hey, you're about to let a small, furry creature jump on your face every morning at five as part of following some path to self-actualization. I don't think you are in any place to make accusations about odd behaviour."

"Cats don't jump on your face!"

"But kittens sure do," said Helene as the doors closed, eclipsing the alarmed face of her friend.

Helene returned to the newsroom and spent the afternoon writing up a story about a new bike lane proposed for a busy road in Victoria. It was sure to create tension between drivers trying to get to work quickly and cyclists hoping to get home alive. Helene considered it a mark of good journalism when she managed to annoy people on both sides of an issue.

Helene liked to leave work just after 5:00 so she could tune in to the last hour of the station's afternoon show while driving. She enjoyed listening to the radio in the car, the patter of discussion a perfect complement to the darkening sky. But the host had just gotten through the weather forecast when Helene's Bluetooth phone cut into the broadcast. The journalist saw from the caller ID that it was Alex again. Preparing to ask how the kitten pickup had gone, she didn't get the opportunity.

"I don't feel well," Alex slurred into the phone. "I just threw up. My stomach is very mad at me."

It took less than a heartbeat for Helene to switch into the role she played when her own children were going through an emergency. Her transformation was faster than a superhero donning a cape in a telephone booth.

"Is your throat closing? What did you just eat? Do you feel cold?" Her instinct was to assume her friend was having an allergic reaction, which usually happened in minutes or even seconds after ingestion. Over the phone she could hear a bang like something heavy hitting the ground.

"I decided to sit down. Well, lie down to be more accurate. The floor seemed safer." Her friend made no attempt to answer the questions she had been asked.

Helene checked that there was no one driving in the right lane, then turned the wheel sharply and pulled into a parking spot.

"Listen Alex, I am going to put you on hold and call an ambulance. But don't hang up. I will be right back. Just stay on the floor and stay on the phone."

"I'll stay on the floor," Alex agreed.

In response to the unfolding emergency, Helene once again felt her actions become automatic. She called 911 and while on the line scrolled through her phone to find her friend's address. She would have kept talking to the dispatcher but she wanted to check on Alex. However, when she tried to switch the connection, she was met with the beeping of a disconnected call. At that point she pulled back into traffic and drove as quickly and safely as possible in the direction of Alex's home.

Helene was relieved and slightly terrified that the ambulance had already reached Alex's apartment building by the time she arrived. The sight of the flashing lights removed any possibility that there had been some kind of misunderstanding over the phone. The journalist did her best to push down the rising panic as memories of her children going through life-threatening anaphylaxis replayed in her mind.

She reached the front doors of the building just in time to hold them open for the emergency responders who were urgently pushing the gurney carrying Alex down the hallway. Her friend had an oxygen mask strapped over her face and her eyes were fluttering open and closed. Helene got permission from the paramedics to ride in the ambulance, leaving her car parked on the street.

After the ambulance arrived at the hospital, Alex was taken away by doctors for immediate medical attention. Finding a quiet corner in the busy waiting room, Helene first called her children, instructing them to have leftovers for dinner. She then collapsed into an uncomfortable chair where she anxiously waited for news of her friend's condition.

Being surrounded by the sallow green walls of the hospital brought back memories of the countless visits Helene had made with her children to the ER when they were very young. For the first few years of her daughter's life, Helene wasn't able to easily judge which allergic reactions were life-threatening, or which would just cause hives. This meant she and Cleo had made the frantic trip to the hospital at least once a month. That was one of the reasons she perpetually carried a water bottle and snacks in her backpack — she never wanted to be at the mercy of a hospital vending machine for nourishment, especially when they were stocked with food that wasn't even safe for her kids to eat. By the time her son came along, Helene had a better understanding of when a reaction was severe or not, or when a situation could be resolved with antihistamines and a shower to remove any traces of the allergen from the skin. But he had still experienced anaphylaxis three times before reaching his tenth birthday, so she was always prepared to spend hours in the hospital while doctors repeatedly administered epinephrine into the impossibly thin arms of her terrified child.

Waiting for word of her friend's condition in the early evening, Helene was unable to focus on reading or watching anything on her phone, so she passed several hours by observing the struggling patients and their worried families. One confused elderly woman, perhaps in the first stages of dementia, clung to the hand of her reassuring husband with the terror of a frightened child. Her eyes grew wide with alarm whenever a new person entered the area. Another actual child lay on their mother's lap, nursing an injured arm, too exhausted to even make any kind of complaint. Helene was grateful her own offspring were safe at home. Even the assumption that they were probably playing video games instead of doing their homework gave her comfort rather than concern.

"You came in with Alex Chang?" A young doctor asked as he approached Helene.

"Yes, she's my friend. Friend and colleague. But mostly friend." Helene decided to stop talking as she was borderline delirious.

"The good news is, we've stabilized her, but we still don't know exactly what's wrong. We're going to have to run some toxicology tests. You don't know if she ingested drugs, do you?"

"Drugs? Alex? No. I've never known her to do anything like that. She is really more of a whisky person. Are you saying she took drugs?" Helene hoped that experimenting with illicit substances was not a part of Alex's new approach to embracing life. But she was also aware that many people who lost loved ones to an overdose didn't even know their family member or friend consumed drugs.

100

"It's just one possibility, and, like I said, we'll need to run some tests."

"But will she be okay?"

"We're going to take good care of her. But right now you should probably go home. You can call us in the morning to see how she's doing." The doctor was just about to turn and walk away when he added, "By the way, while she was in and out of consciousness, she mentioned something about a new kitten. Does she have a pet? Are you able to check on it?"

Despite the seriousness of the situation, Helene smiled weakly in response to his question. She really hadn't expected her duties as a godparent to a kitten to kick in quite so soon.

Chapter 14

Less than 48 hours after leaving the hospital, Helene found herself in a different kind of waiting room. It too had chairs that punished you for sitting, and the space held a similar fetid air of despondency. There was also a sense of impending bad news. On that Wednesday morning in the Victoria police station, a person might be fearing spending time in a jail cell, whereas in the emergency room, a cancer diagnosis could be the source of dread.

Helene was grateful she didn't have to wait long before a uniformed officer indicated the journalist should follow her down a beige hallway with pockmarked walls. After a short walk, she was deposited alone in an interview room, the door clicking loudly upon closing, ominously locking from the outside. She assumed she had been called to the police station as a consequence of her friend's sudden illness.

The journalist had taken the previous day off work to tend to her friend. She had brought a bag of plain food, including crackers and yogurt, to the hospital, hoping it would entice Alex to eat. But at the sight of the food, the writer had just shaken her head weakly, her skin still painted an ashen hue. So, Helene had settled for keeping her friend company, even as the patient napped every few hours.

During one of her waking moments, Alex did ask about the new kitten that Helene had collected from her friend's apartment, along with a stash of unopened cat paraphernalia. Helene's own children were delighted by the arrival of the small furry creature, taking turns holding it on their lap. Helene wasn't sure they were listening when she repeatedly stated that their small visitor was only on loan, like a library book that purred.

In the morning, when Helene had tried to get information from the doctors about what had caused her friend's collapse, she at first was told they were still waiting on the test results. But by the afternoon she sensed the doctors were hiding something — they had become stern and tight-lipped when she continued to inquire about the cause of the illness. Only a casual encounter with a nurse shed any light on the situation. She had asked the man in blue scrubs if he expected Alex to have an appetite any time soon, and he had said that it always took a while for people to eat after a poisoning. The suggestion of suspicious circumstances meant Helene was not particularly surprised when she received a call early the next morning from Detective Kalinowski to come down to the station for a "chat." The officer sounded distinctly less chummy than on previous occasions.

"It appears people keep dying around you." Detective Kalinowski once again dispensed with the niceties of conversation after walking into the interview room, placing her notepad and coffee cup on the table.

Helene was momentarily silenced by the shock of the detective's statement, but then responded with rising panic, "My friend isn't dead. And she isn't going to die. Unless there is something you aren't telling me!"

The detective had the decency to look a bit abashed at the alarm she had caused. "No. It appears she will be okay. At least that's what the doctors say. But they also tell me it could have been much worse."

"Do they know what it was? Was it something she ate?"

"You are here to answer my questions, not the other way around," stated the detective.

Helene sensed the quid pro quo relationship they had previously developed was now over, although the detective did add, "But eating something is the most likely way she was poisoned."

The journalist sat back to take this news in. It was one thing to have a nurse accidentally mention a possible poisoning, but it was quite another to hear it from a senior detective of the Victoria Police Department.

After giving Helene a moment to process this information, Kalinowski got down to business. "Now, I need to know when you saw your friend on Monday. What you did together, and what she ate, if anything."

Helene cast her mind back to the start of the week, how refreshed she had felt coming to work in the morning. It all seemed like a distant memory after the harrowing experiences of the past two days.

She described to the detective how Alex had stopped off at her work without warning to announce the news she was adopting a kitten. She then shared her friend's request for Helene to be a sort of godparent to the new pet. However, when Helene mentioned the box of chocolates Alex had ferried from reception, the detective looked up from her notebook.

"Where did the chocolates come from?"

"I don't know. There was no note. Just my name was on them."

"Do you usually get chocolates delivered to the station?"

"This was the first time. Although we do get cookies and pies from communication companies at Christmas. A sort of thank you for occasionally paying attention to their press releases."

"And did you eat the chocolates?"

Detective Kalinowski hardly seemed to need to breathe between questions. Helene was doing her best to keep up.

"No. They had nuts. The chocolates. I always check because my children are allergic."

"But you aren't? Allergic, that is?"

"No, but what if they get on my lips, and then that gets on my water bottle, and then my children take a drink? It's how I live. I have to be so careful."

"Where are the chocolates now?"

Helene had to pause to recall this information. "I was in a hurry to get back to work. I put them in a drawer. To give away later."

"Are they still there?"

"I assume so. I mean, I haven't been back since I went to the hospital with Alex on Monday evening. Do you want me to call my producer to find them?"

Detective Kalinowski appeared to consider her answer. "No, I think it's better we send an officer. To protect any fingerprints. I'll be back in a minute."

Sitting alone in the police interview room while Kalinowski arranged for the suspicious gift to be retrieved from her work desk, Helene tried to comprehend the confirmation that her friend had been poisoned, possibly by a box of chocolates intended for her. And that, in some ironic twist of fate, her children's allergy to nuts had possibly saved her life.

By the time Detective Kalinowski had returned to the room, Helene had decided to share everything she had learned in her investigation into the murder of Lucy Marino. She could only assume that she had unknowingly stumbled across a killer and they were determined to silence her. As Helene launched into a detailed record of the people she had talked to over the past week, Kalinowski furiously scribbled the details in a notebook.

The florist who lied about knowing Lucy Marino.

The art professor who sent hate mail to his former student.

A sister who had been cheated out of an inheritance.

Helene had to give the detective credit for not being angrier with the journalist for holding back information.

Kalinowski was like a parent who knew the child's shame was punishment enough. And Helene was also going to have to find a way to live with the guilt of her friend being poisoned. She was only slightly ashamed to admit to herself that the thought of her own death, which would have left her children motherless, scared her the most.

"What do I do now?" the journalist asked the detective, feeling utterly exhausted after what seemed like a lengthy confession of sins.

"First we have to confirm the poison was in the chocolates," replied Kalinowski.

"And if it turns out someone was actually trying to kill me?"

"I am going to have to solve the murder of Marino. That must be the connection. Unless you are working on another story that has made someone very angry."

Helene knew that people were passionate about dog parks and bike lanes in Victoria, but she didn't think they would resort to poisoning. Vitriolic op-eds in the local newspaper were normally how they attacked their opponents.

"No. It must be someone I spoke to about Marino." At this point Helen feared the detective would swear her off any more meddling, but she thought it was worth a try. "What can I do to help? I want to find out who did this to my friend."

"I think you already have, by uncovering some good leads. I knew about the sister and the inheritance, but the art school stuff is worth following up on. But you need to stop blundering around. Check with me before you speak to any of these people again. Remember, you have a target on your back. And right now, I think you should just go home and tell your kids to be extra careful for the next few days. Don't go to the mall after school."

Even the fleeting thought of Oscar and Cleo coming to harm made Helene feel nauseated. But she knew her children wouldn't be safe until the killer was caught. Sitting in the uncomfortable metal chair in the cheerless police interview room, Helene desperately wished she had never gone for a walk on the breakwater on the fateful evening when she discovered the body of Lucy Marino. But regret was too small a word for how she felt.

Assuming she was allowed to leave, Helene stood up and slung her backpack over her shoulder.

"By the way," asked the detective in a tone that sounded like an afterthought but probably wasn't, "you don't have a heart condition, do you?"

"No," answered Helene.

"Or take any heart medication?"

"Why would I take heart medication if I don't have problems with my heart?"

"We can check, you know," warned the detective, "on your prescriptions."

"Feel free," said Helene. "But I don't understand why you are asking. Is this something to do with what made Alex sick?"

"It was digitalis, what your friend ingested. A common medication, but she got a toxic dose."

When Detective Kalinowski mentioned the digitalis, a connection tickled Helene's brain, but in the most maddening of ways it dangled just out of reach of her conscious thoughts. She forced her mind to move on, knowing any insight would probably occur while she was performing a mundane task like washing her hair.

Helene decided not to return to the hospital after she was done at the police station as Alex's parents had arrived in town and were at the bedside of their daughter. They probably had many questions for Helene about why their only child had been poisoned, and the journalist wasn't up for a second grilling that day. So she went to the radio station instead but couldn't concentrate on work. When she told her producer that she would take another day of leave to recover from the incident, Riya didn't object — it was a slow day in the newsroom.

With memories of the police interview replaying in her mind on the drive home, Helene knew she desperately needed a walk on the breakwater. The ocean wind would hopefully wash away the general sense of grubbiness that came from spending time in a room normally inhabited by criminals.

There was no cruise ship in the harbour, so the breakwater was mercifully less busy than usual. However, Helene felt such a deep longing for solitude that she decided to walk on the lower granite level of the structure, in the hopes of avoiding people entirely.

Leaping from one block to another, Helene had to take care with her footing as the tide was coming in and high waves had left pools of water on the uneven surface. When the wind picked up, occasional waves crashed against the side of the pathway, sending up a spray which Helene found refreshing rather than threatening. She didn't mind getting a bit wet. It helped her to concentrate on physical sensations rather than useless repetitive thoughts about what had happened and what might still happen — the past and future tugging like two bullies, both trying to steal her peace of mind.

While Helene was watching the horizon for any possible orca sightings to report to her son, Lee appeared on the path in front of her. Although she had not been seeking company on her breakwater excursion, the appearance of the Coast Guard officer was welcome. In his Cowichan sweater, and with his distant gaze, he seemed to be part of the ocean environment rather than a human intruder. Sensing her approach, he turned and smiled warmly.

"Just keeping an eye on the boats," Lee stated, as if apologizing for intruding on her walk.

"Isn't it hard to see from here?" Helene was only able to distinguish the faint outlines of small vessels in the distance.

"After so many years, I know them well. Like a watcher of the sky who knows the difference between a star and a planet."

As they stood side by side on the granite blocks, the sun began to slip behind the horizon, lighting up the clouds with a thousand shades of lilac, like a final spirited farewell. It reminded Helene of her favourite poem by Dylan Thomas, *Do not go gentle into that good night.*

The journalist wondered if the curator had fought back against death, her life draining like the colours from the sky at close of day. Or perhaps the gunshot wound had made her death mercifully quick. Helene could only hope so.

"Look at the purple, almost like a camas flower in spring." Lee pointed to a bright solitary cloud above the mountains. A splash of paint on a canvas of sky.

A flower.

A toxic bloom.

The petals of the foxglove.

There is perhaps no sensation more satisfying to the human brain than making a connection that had eluded discovery, an epiphany lured from the shadows.

Lee had mentioned the camas flower, a plant local Indigenous communities had eaten and traded for millennia. And the plant still bloomed each spring in the meadows of Beacon Hill Park. However, there were two types of camas: the edible purple one, and a white one that was toxic to humans. This got Helene thinking about the digitalis poisoning of her friend. It wasn't white camas that contained the drug, but another lilac-coloured flower that grew in Victoria. The bell-shaped foxglove flower was as beautiful as it was deadly — a source of digitalis.

As the journalist considered the possibility that someone had used foxglove to poison her friend, she realized there were now two floral connections to the curator's murder — the other being the dandelion traces in Marino's wound. Helene couldn't help but wonder if this was further proof that the cagey florist was mixed up in the murder.

With thoughts of deadly blossoms front of mind, Helene could no longer stand and muse at the ocean. She said her goodbyes to Lee, who simply nodded in return.

The journalist took no notice of the colours jousting in the sky as the sunset waned. She walked with a brisk pace and purpose, knowing each step might be taking her closer to catching a killer.

March 7, 1886

My dearest Constance,

The past few weeks have been filled with such frantic activity, making me guilty of neglecting our correspondence. I am preparing for an exhibition of my work at a hall owned by a patron who has made his fortune in coal. He is one of those rare men of commerce with a profound esteem for the arts. He has already acquired several of my larger works.

You would be most shocked to learn that I have been spending the hours, from waking to sleeping, framing and hanging my many canvases. The scrapes and cuts adorning my hands bear testimony to my industrious labour. I know it is work I should leave to the carpenter, but I am so disquieted when a frame is not well suited to a painting over which I have toiled for weeks.

I am almost feverish with excitement as the opening of the exhibit grows ever closer. I could only wish you were able to be in attendance. My friend Margaret is helping to organize the soirée, and even though I know I should be grateful, I must admit her presence is a poor substitute for your sympathetic company.

When I need a moment to myself, away from all the preparations, I have been taking calming walks along the water's edge. The fresh and salty air does wash away my worries like they were old paint on a brush. I know you would not approve, but last week I fell into happy conversation with a fisherman who was hauling his boat onto the shore. We talked for more than one quarter of an *hour just about the patterns of light on the rolling waves. It was the most delightful and easiest of exchanges.*

Sometimes I do wonder whether I would have been better born a peasant, so naturally do I break the rules meant to apply to people of our rank. But perhaps artists belong to no class and to every class of people. And that is both the gift and hardship of the creative soul.

I am sorry to learn that your lungs are still causing you continued difficulty. Perhaps your travels to the countryside will bring some relief. Please send more news of how your own plans for the coming weeks are unfolding. I envy your tour of the Lake District, for as much as I have grown fond of the flora of my adopted country, the sight of purple heathers on the moors would bring such comfort. Perhaps my dear niece or nephew could sketch a scene from your travels for their distant aunt.

With steadfast affection,

   Amelia

Chapter 15

"I want the light from the window to pick out the turquoise of the ocean. Can you turn it to the left, *un peu*, Helene?"

Over the last 24 hours, Helene had found herself demoted from a successful radio journalist to a brow-beaten photographer's assistant.

After conferring with Detective Kalinowski about the possibility that the digitalis had come from a foxglove flower, the journalist shared that she was going to keep working on her feature story about the newly discovered paintings. The two of them agreed that if the journalist focused solely on the work of Amelia Grayson and not the death of Lucy Marino, she shouldn't be putting herself in too much more danger. However, she had been warned to only eat food she had prepared herself in case the poisoner tried again. Helene didn't bother to explain that, due to extreme allergies, her family already assumed many foods might kill them.

The journalist had been informed, when she arrived at work on Wednesday, that the national news team was interested in doing a TV and web piece on the two paintings by Grayson. Apparently, the discovery of unknown works by 19th century Canadian artists was 21st century clickbait. Helene was thrilled her story would be broadcast across the country, but she also knew it probably meant editorial interference from media executives in Toronto.

The first indication that her concerns about losing control over the story were well founded was when a photojournalist from Quebec showed up one morning. He had swept into the newsroom wearing distressed jeans, a black turtleneck and a cashmere scarf. He looked more like a model who posed in front of cameras rather than the artist behind one.

Although Helene had no formal training in photography, she was usually allowed to take the pictures for her own stories. But apparently Jean-Pierre Manet was specially commissioned to capture images of the two landscape paintings, a skill he made clear no amateur should attempt. From the moment of his arrival, he also appeared to be under the impression that Helene was tasked to do his bidding. The journalist had never found it quite so annoying to hear her name called out with the correct French pronunciation, with a silent H.

"Helene!" barked the photographer dramatically, "I said *plus à gauche*, not to the right. Must I do it all for myself?"

Helene moved the painting in the other direction, thinking that if this abuse continued, Detective Kalinowski was going to have another murder to investigate.

Finally appearing to be satisfied with the composition and light, Jean-Pierre rapidly snapped photos of the ocean landscape set up on an easel in Grayson's studio. Helene stepped out of the room in the hopes of getting a break from the photojournalist's relentless nagging. It was also a chance to go over her checklist of the people she needed to interview for her radio piece about the paintings.

Helene had already recorded the museum archivist explaining how the paint and the canvases of the two landscapes had been analyzed to ensure they matched the chemical composition of other works by Amelia Grayson. The staff member detailed the way Grayson mixed specific colours in oils that were absolutely unique. She finished by describing how the discovery of the paintings was bringing welcome attention to the Victorian artist and the museum itself. There was even talk of a national touring exhibit in the fall, including a stop at the National Gallery in Ottawa.

Helene knew her piece needed the voice of an art historian who could highlight Grayson's importance as an early Canadian painter, especially at a time when men dominated the salons and galleries. However, much to her dismay, when she did a quick internet search for experts, the name of Professor Neumann, from the art college, was at the top of the list. She cringed at the thought of speaking to the arrogant academic in argyle again.

Helene knew she should let Detective Kalinowski know she might interview the professor, because of his connection to the murder investigation, but her call to the police officer went straight to voicemail. The journalist decided to go ahead and contact the academic, rationalizing that she could share the recording of her interview with the detective.

Jean-Pierre was still busy taking pictures of the paintings in Grayson's studio, so Helene made her way downstairs to a quiet room off the main gallery. The last thing she needed was for her call to be interrupted by the demands of the photographer — she was going to have to have her wits about her when speaking to Neumann. Before dialling the main number for the art college, Helene took a seat on an antique upholstered chair built during an era when furniture was valued for elegance not comfort. She wondered if Grayson herself had visited the room often but decided the poor light from a single north-facing window probably meant she didn't.

Helene's call first went through to the main campus reception and was then transferred to Neumann's office line. Helene expected to leave a voicemail, as most people rarely answered landlines anymore. However, being an expert in Canadian 19th century artists may have meant Neumann was a bit of a Luddite, as the phone rang only once before the handset was picked up.

"Professor Neumann speaking." The brittle upper-class British accent made Helene wonder if the academic had missed his calling as an actor in Edwardian dramas for public television.

"Hello, this is Helene Unger from Vancouver Island Radio. We met last week."

If the academic's tone had started off slightly chilly, it now dipped to subarctic. "Are you the one who sent the police after me? Had them rifling through my possessions, as if I were a common criminal, and asking questions about expensive chocolates? I am quite sure I have nothing to say to you."

Helene was caught off guard. She hadn't expected Kalinowski to have already followed up with the professor.

"I know the police are making their own inquiries into Lucy Marino's death, but I think they are simply speaking to everyone who once knew her." Helene couldn't pretend that her explanation didn't sound weak.

"And are they accusing everyone of sending her hate mail?"

"I didn't know about that," lied Helene, realizing this conversation was headed in the direction she had promised the detective she would avoid.

"I had to explain to them that I had *received* the vile messages, not sent them. I had only kept them in case I needed to make a report to the police. They took all the letters away for analysis, and I had to give a DNA sample to test for saliva on the envelopes. Quite the most humiliating experience, to be sure."

Helene's mind raced in reaction to this new information.

Why had both Neumann and Marino gotten hate mail?

What had inspired the vicious messages?

Did this mean the professor was not a murderer?

Deciding she needed to take back control of the conversation, Helene pressed on. "I am not calling about the investigation into Lucy Marino's murder, but rather the two Amelia Grayson paintings she discovered. I am doing a

116

story for national news, and I understand you are an expert on her legacy and work."

As she expected, the promise of being featured in a story that would get national coverage caused the academic to quickly regain his composure. She could tell that his concerns about being a suspect in a police investigation had been supplanted by thoughts of acclaim for his brilliant opinions. Raised in the milieu of a highly competitive university campus, Helene knew that no academic would miss an opportunity to expound upon their theories and research. The vanity of a viral online influencer could not compete with the hubris of a recently quoted professor.

"Where would you like to start?" asked the professor, who now sounded much more compliant.

"I assume you have seen photographs of the paintings?" began Helene, making note of the time code on the phone recorder so she could quickly locate the start of material she could quote from.

"Yes, in fact, I had the chance to inspect them in person. I was one of the experts who was hired to authenticate the paintings."

This was welcome news to Helene, who knew his comments would carry extra weight in the story.

"So, what do you make of them?"

"To begin with, the style and subject is unmistakably Grayson. The brush strokes, the way she captures the sun reflecting off the dewy meadow with the clarity of morning light. In fact, the manner in which she creates the texture of the bark on the Douglas Fir trees has never been replicated by another artist. A mixture of light and dark pigments that brings life to the canvas." Neumann was hitting his stride, and Helene could now imagine herself one of his students in a lecture hall frantically taking notes.

"I also believe this particular tree was a favourite of the artist. Having come from England at a young age, where the best sort of trees was to be found on the estates of the aristocrats, the grandeur of the species of the North American conifer left a mark on her psyche."

Helene recalled a phrase from one of Grayson's letters, *a muted giant of the wood.*

"But what about the ocean scene, with what appears to be a fisherman? I understand this is the only time she included a figure in a landscape."

Neumann took a dramatic pause before answering, like an actor who knew he had an audience in thrall.

"I have to admit, the inclusion of the human form did at first give me cause for doubt. Why would the artist pursue this new approach? And why a solitary fisherman? It raised many questions to which I do not have answers. However, ultimately, I had to remind myself that many artists change direction during their career. Renoir abandoned the avant-garde experimentation of impressionism for the strictures of the old masters. The first works of Van Gogh were dark and haunted by shadows, whereas *The Starry Night* is dancing with light and form. So, after the brush work and paint composition were all thoroughly investigated in Grayson's paintings, I finally felt comfortable confirming the authenticity of them both."

"But what do you make of the fact that the individual who donated the paintings wants to stay anonymous?"

"It is disappointing, of course, as it would allow us to better establish the provenance of the works, but these things happen. The world of art is dominated by the wealthy elite, and their dealings are not always strictly legal. I can appreciate their desire to avoid a spotlight on how they acquired the art. It could result in a dispute over ownership."

"But they have donated the art to the museum — surely money is not the issue now," Helene probed further.

"It is not a matter of money but rather a matter of reputation. The rich guard their family's legacy, trying to shed any associations with slavery or colonialism. And the story of art contains more crimes than the diamond trade."

118

Now that Helene had what she needed from her interview, she decided to pursue a line of questioning that wasn't strictly related to the paintings.

"Just one last thing. You have admitted that there was no love lost between yourself and the late curator, Lucy Marino. Why did she choose you to authenticate the paintings?"

"She didn't. I was contacted by the archivist, and all my dealings were through her." The professor has lost his effusive tone, and his reply was short and guarded.

"Isn't that a little odd?"

"Perhaps, but I can only imagine Marino wanted to avoid contact as well, knowing I probably wouldn't have responded to her request."

"But why you? Aren't there other art historians they could have used?"

"Not one who has the same breadth of understanding. You see, my PhD thesis was largely based on the works of Grayson, 'The use of light in 19th century West Coast landscapes.'"

Helene keenly wanted to ask the academic if he knew how Marino had gotten her job as a curator, since she didn't even graduate from the art institute. But she expected this would definitely count as interfering in the police investigation. Instead, she thanked him for his time and ended the call.

"Helene! Helene!" Just as she was about to check the quality of the phone recording, the journalist heard Jean-Pierre calling from the corridor. He reminded her of a parent trying to track down a wayward child.

Packing up her gear, Helene made her way back into the main part of the museum.

When the photographer spotted her, he came rushing over with his camera.

"I must show you the shots I have made this day, to know if you are pleased with them." The photographer's tone had shed its haughty arrogance and instead had a note of yearning for approval.

He passed the camera to the journalist, showing her how to click through the digital photos he had taken.

An easel caught in a blade of the sun.

The warm tones of the scarred wooden floor.

A studio vibrant with life despite the artist's death a century ago.

"*Magnifique!*" Helene declared as she passed the camera back to Jean-Pierre. Her earlier resentment of the photographer had been replaced by respect for his talent. He was undoubtedly a gifted artist, and Helene knew this demanded a certain allowance for the temperament of a fragile ego.

Both artists and academics used arrogance to mask an insatiable longing for praise. But whether it was an art historian, a baker or a talented florist, Helene knew her job was to authenticate the person, as though they themselves were a painting, revealing the provenance and pitfalls of their soul.

Chapter 16

As she held the cupboard door open with one hand, Helene scanned the shelves from left to right. Egg noodles, spaghetti noodles, vermicelli, penne, wonton, udon and even something called indomie which, according to the label, came from Indonesia. Her friend's pantry was a veritable international dictionary of pasta. But while the cupboard was replete with various shapes of starch, when it came to vegetables there were only two cans of mushrooms and a glass jar of marinated artichokes. Helene wondered if the two preserved vegetables would be eaten in the same meal or on separate occasions. Neither variation of the menu was particularly appealing.

"I guess you aren't a follower of the low-carb diet," Helene called to Alex, who was lying on the couch with a pink fleece blanket tucked around her body. A small black kitten was curled up on her lap like a furry paper weight.

"I have never met a noodle I didn't like. And they don't go off like a carton of strawberries you forgot in the back of your fridge. Fruit is just a waste of money, if you ask me."

Helene had picked up her friend from the hospital that morning. The doctors felt her recovery was far enough along that she could now rest at home, but they wanted someone to check on Alex once a day. The writer's parents had already returned to Kelowna — apparently their Shih Tzu, who was boarding at a dog kennel, was refusing all food. So once their daughter had started to nibble on crackers, they decided the stomach of their four-legged patient needed them more.

"Are you sure I can't pick up something else from the grocery store? I think the doctors said yogurt would help restore your gut bacteria."

"Yogurt is just ice cream without the good bits. Speaking of which, ice cream does sound yummy. Chocolate banana chunk if you can find it. I don't mind fruit in desserts."

Helene shook her head and wondered how she could have known Alex for so many years but managed to remain ignorant of her dietary idiosyncrasies. Perhaps because they typically went out for drinks together, not food.

"Do you need some sauces for your pasta? I can pick them up as well as the ice cream."

"Sauce just masks the flavour of the noodle. I prefer butter and salt," replied Alex. "I'm a purist."

Opening the fridge door, Helene was relieved to see a couple of fresh, if slightly wilted, vegetables and a jar of all-natural peanut butter. She wouldn't rule out buying some fruit, despite the objections. She was too much of a mother not to. It would just have to be a kind that didn't go bad quickly, like pears or apples.

"Can I make you a cup of tea before I go?"

Helene would admit that taking care of her friend was one way to assuage her guilt over the poisoning. She desperately wished she had never gotten Alex involved in the murder investigation.

"If you can just make sure the kitten has fresh water and food, that'd be great. And there are some papers for you on the kitchen table."

Curious about what her friend could possibly be referring to, Helene surveyed the surface of the table that was used as a repository for everything from gym gear to recycling.

"It's the will of Lucy Marino's mother," Alex explained while stroking the kitten's head gently. "I made a copy when

122

I looked it up for you. Maybe it'll help you figure out who did this to me."

Helene had opened her mouth to apologize again for everything that had happened, but Alex raised a hand to silence her.

"It's not your fault. You didn't poison me. And if anything, it's just a cautionary tale about what can happen when you eat other people's chocolates," Alex said with false levity. Then she stated with an utterly serious tone, "But you do need to catch the bastard. Daisy and I are counting on you."

It took Helene a moment to figure out that her friend was referring to the cat as Daisy. She hadn't realized Alex had named the creature already. She wasn't sure why someone would name an entirely black cat after a white-and-yellow flower. Maybe digitalis poisoning had some odd side effects on the brain.

Helene waited until she was sitting in her car before looking at the will her friend had printed up. As Alex had noted, there was a codicil stating that if anything happened to Lucy in the five years after inheriting, the estate would go to Paola. Perhaps their mother had some vestiges of guilt for leaving everything to one daughter. Helene also noticed that the address for the house in question was practically on her drive home.

Turning left instead of right at the end of the street, Helene felt only a twinge of trepidation. Although she had promised Detective Kalinowski she would clear any actions connected with the investigation in advance, Alex's demand to discover the culprit was still fresh in her mind. She needed to catch the bastard.

It was a quiet drive to Moss Bay, still too early in the afternoon for the heavier traffic of people heading home from work or school. The sun was high in a cloudless sky, showing off the glory of Victoria in mid-March. Fruit trees blushed with blossoms, and fresh grass turned yards into lush green carpets. While the rest of the country still fought winter with shovels and snowplows, southern Vancouver Island was going through a botanical renewal. There was a reason many Canadians dreamed of retiring to the coastal city, exchanging their winter boots for garden clogs. And when there was the occasional rare snowfall, most people just hid in their homes until it had melted.

Arriving on the street where the mother's property was located, Helene slowed her car down to a crawl as she scanned the house numbers. Most of the homes were in the wooden arts-and-crafts style from the first few decades of the 20th century. They were well cared for, with tastefully painted window frames and manicured lawns. Some even boasted wraparound porches, conjuring up warm summer afternoons and jugs of iced tea. They were like dollhouses from an idyllic childhood, homes to the wealthy whose dreams had come true.

In the end, it wasn't a house number that caught Helene's attention, but instead a giant dumpster in a front yard. She ducked down in the seat when she saw Lucy Marino's sister, Paola, chucking a pile of papers into the oversized container. The legs of an overturned chair could be seen sticking out of the top of the receptacle like the feet of a dead bird in one of her son's cartoons.

Helene drove a little farther along, turned the car around, and then parked a short distance down the street. She still had a good view of the activities taking place on the front lawn of the house due to the neighbour's very low and neatly trimmed hedge. Settling into the front seat of the car, Helene kept her sunglasses on. She figured that if she was going to act the part of a private investigator, she might as well look like one.

Helene could only imagine what the affluent neighbours thought of the presence of the dented dumpster that dominated the front lawn like a crude, alien spaceship. If they didn't like strangers' cars parked in front of their

124

homes in Moss Bay, they certainly weren't going to appreciate a garbage bin better suited to a construction site.

About twenty minutes passed without any more activity in the yard, and Helene was beginning to think the whole exercise might be a waste of time. But finally, Paola emerged from the house again, carrying a large box of papers. She dumped out the contents and then went back into the building. Staying inside for only a few minutes, the baker emerged wearing a faded yellow raincoat, in spite of the sunshine. She proceeded to drive away in a dilapidated compact, the muffler giving off an unhealthy rumble.

At this point Helene went through a short internal debate about what to do next. As a journalist and a friend seeking justice, she saw an opportunity to possibly uncover vital clues that might help solve a murder and a poisoning. But as someone who recently spent time in a hospital and a police interview room, fearing for the safety of her loved ones, she also had a strong impulse to start the car and drive straight home. She reconciled herself to following the riskier path with the belief that the sooner the killer was caught, the sooner life could go back to normal.

Helene left her backpack in the car as she didn't want to carry any extra weight before attempting what might be a physically challenging manoeuvre. However, when she walked up to the dumpster, she realized its height would make it impossible to simply leap over the side. A quick search of the backyard revealed a short ladder, probably used for picking apples in the fall. Helene placed the steps next to the weathered container, climbed up, and swung her leg over the side. Thankfully there was enough discarded material piled up inside so she had a place to land; if the dumpster had been mostly empty, it would have made a long fall to a hard bottom.

Inside the container there was a jumble of broken furniture, dated kitchen appliances, art in garish frames and piles of loose paper and documents. Oddly, there was also a very expensive-looking neon orange life jacket, the kind worn by wealthy folks who owned yachts. Helene somehow had never imagined the curator as a boating enthusiast.

After steadying her footing in the dumpster, Helene lifted up one of the many paintings for closer examination. It turned out to be an image of a young woman sitting at a wooden table, sunlight beaming from an open window creating strong shadows reminiscent of Rembrandt. The woman's features were aquiline and arrogant in the manner of a 17th century European aristocrat. However, the painting was obviously modern, as a pack of cigarettes and a lighter occupied one corner of the table. Helene imagined this was one of Lucy's creations, a mimicry of the style of the master painter but with a crude inclusion of modern objects. The journalist had to admit that the late curator had possessed incredible talent, but there was a certain crassness behind the intention of the painting, as though trying to debase the works of the masters.

Fishing out a few other paintings from the pile, Helene realized they were all done in the style of a particularly well-known artist, including one resembling Warhol's famous Campbell soup. The tin can depicted on this canvas held preserved mushrooms, and it crossed Helene's mind to salvage it for Alex since it matched the contents of her pantry.

It was evident to Helene that Paola was clearing the house of all objects connected to her sister. There was an undeniable anger to the hasty method of disposal, especially considering the quality of the unusual art. Helene knew that as the curator had died just over a week ago, probate wouldn't have passed, and there was no way the baker had the legal right to discard of property in this way. Knowing Paola shouldn't be throwing out paintings and papers made Helene feel a little less guilty about sifting through them without permission.

The journalist started to dig through the documents, looking for anything of significance. Loose receipts showed the curator enjoyed eating out at expensive restaurants and engaging in activities meant for visitors, like tours of botanical gardens and whale-watching expeditions. There was a bag full of fading instruction manuals for appliances, probably the same ones unceremoniously discarded in the dumpster. She had just found a beige folder stuffed with photographs when the noise of an approaching car caught the journalist's attention. With horror, she recognized the growl of the muffler as belonging to the sister's car which had driven off 15 minutes ago. When the engine cut out directly in front of the house, Helene's fears were confirmed.

The journalist had placed the short ladder at the back of the dumpster, on the side facing away from the street, so there was a chance the sister wouldn't see it on her way into the house. However, it was impossible to imagine she would miss the garden steps when she came back down the path. After throwing herself down on a lumpy pile, pushing aside an old kitchen mixer that was digging into her stomach, Helene lay still and listened to the sound of Paola's footsteps as she walked from the car and then ascended the front porch. She waited just over a minute to make sure the sister was out of sight before scrambling back to her knees.

Grabbing a worn reusable shopping bag half-buried in the mess, Helene began stuffing random papers into the bag. Photos, documents, notebooks — she would have to sort through it all later. With regret, she acknowledged there was no way she could easily and quietly get the paintings out of the dumpster, so she left them to ultimately be buried in a landfill. But as she glanced around for any last items to salvage, she did spot a box of paints, the colours rich and luminous. Her own children could make use of the art supplies, and maybe it was a small way to carry on the curator's legacy.

Just as she was about to heft her leg over the side wall of the dumpster and make her escape, Helene spotted a bundle of white petals in the corner. It was the pricey bouquet of orchids she had paid Benjamin Cornish to send to Paola Marino. Although the baker had the decency not to throw out the flowers in front of her employees at the bakery where they had been delivered, the woman clearly wanted no memories of her sister, alive or dead. As Helene made a hasty retreat across the lawn to her car, the heavy shopping bag of papers in hand, Helene surmised the sister could use another dumpster to hold all the bitterness in her heart.

March 15, 1886

My dearest Constance,

I do not know where or when this post will find you as I believe your northern journey has long since commenced. I do hope the sun is a faithful companion on your travels, for that lush region of England is known for its occasional damp glory.

I myself do seem to spend less time wandering in nature with the exhibit underway. The opening night was a resplendent gathering of all Victoria's high society, and I believe even the mayor did make a short appearance. I only wonder if the ladies and their gentlemen did attend most eagerly in order to encounter the odd species on display, a painter of the feminine sex. I caught whispers about a woman who absurdly abandoned a life of easy comforts to peddle her art in drawing rooms. My dear sister, I am not so dissimilar from a performing circus animal, and I wouldn't have been at all surprised to have been offered a coin in exchange for a lark with a brush. There was also a moment made most uncomfortable by the arrival of Howard Weatherington, my former fiancé. He has since married, and his wife has borne him three sons, so he can have no complaints in that quarter. But still I could not help feeling his eyes were trailing me as I drifted between the conversations of handsome couples.

Margaret, of course, was also present, as she has provided such tireless effort in organizing the endeavour. Sometimes I feel like I take no small advantage of our friendship, especially as I can so easily tire of her eager company.

However, if the critics are to be taken at their word, the show is an unassailable success, and I have received several more commissions of late. And yet the praise of society does not so fill my heart as you might imagine. It cannot quite compare to the thrill I experience when I show some fresh sketches to the fisherman who I encounter on rare mornings when I catch my breath walking along the water. I feel more honesty in his blunt estimation of my seascape than the baroque praise of the self-important art critic who penned the newspaper review.

As always, I send my love to yourself and to the children. I keenly await drawings from their moorish adventures through the abundant heather.

With steadfast affection,

Amelia

Chapter 17

With her story on the two Grayson paintings almost complete, and the best of Jean-Pierre's photos selected for the web story, Helene had to return to regular work in the newsroom until the opening of the public exhibit at the museum next week. At the morning meeting, when her producer Riya had asked for someone to attend a Coast Guard press conference at 11:00, Helene volunteered. It might give her a chance to say hello to Lee again. She hadn't seen him on any of her breakwater walks of late, and she had to admit she was drawn to his quiet yet reassuring company.

When she arrived at the harbour meeting room where the press conference was being held, the first thing Helene did was plug her mic cord into the group feed. It was the easiest way for the media to collect audio at this kind of event. TV people still had to set up their shot and balance their colours, an extra headache and one of the many reasons Helene had never pursued a career in the visual and superficial medium.

Taking the seat at the end of a row, the journalist gritted her teeth when someone pushed by and took the chair directly next to her. The row in front and behind were completely empty, so there was no excuse for such proximity. It was especially irksome as the man who sat down was one of the more obnoxious members of the press. Gary Graham worked for another radio station, one that traded in opinion more often than fact. The reporter was wearing his trademark vintage Toronto Blue Jays hat and a sneer he must have believed passed for a smile.

"Is there any news on Alex?" Gary asked as though he and Helene were the best of friends rather than rivals who rarely spoke.

Helene kept her expression neutral, not wanting to give anything away. "I am not sure what you are talking about. Is there something I missed?"

"Well, I heard she ended up in hospital a few days ago, although no one appears to know why. We are all very worried."

Helene had to stop herself from releasing a loud guffaw at the idea that Gary Graham was concerned about her friend.

"I am sure if Alex wants her medical concerns to become fodder for social media, she will come straight to you."

Helene was saved from any further conversation with Graham by the entrance of Coast Guard members who stepped onto the platform, indicating the press conference was about to begin. The journalist was disappointed to see the younger officer, Jeff, on the stage, but not his older colleague. Although, when she thought about it, the image of Lee, in his knit Coast Salish hat, putting on a show for the press, seemed completely incongruous to his stoic character.

"Today we wanted to share news of a large joint operation between American and Canadian agencies which has resulted in the seizure of toxic drugs headed for the streets of our communities." Jeff had stepped forward to the microphone and was speaking to the gathering of journalists with the sonorous tones of a Baptist preacher. Helene decided that the Coast Guard had chosen their spokesperson well. Jeff not only had a handsome jawline made for TV but also a resonant voice ideal for radio.

"When officers boarded a small sailboat on the morning of March 2nd, they located more than a kilogram of fentanyl, 250 grams of ketamine and several kilograms of cocaine." Jeff continued describing the stash of drugs seized by the Coast Guard units with obvious pride. Helene could not blame them for trumpeting the news of the drug bust. The government was desperate to prove they were turning the tide on the deadly opioid overdose crisis that was claiming the lives of half a dozen people in the province each day. A public emergency had been declared in the province in 2016, but the deaths were only accelerating among drug users. Over the past few years, Helene had spoken to grieving mothers who had been spurred by their offspring's fatal overdoses to become advocates. These interviews had once again confirmed one of Helene's core beliefs: that there is nothing more devastating to a human soul than the loss of a child.

From the platform, Jeff shared the identities of the individuals arrested in connection with the drug bust as well as estimating the street value of the stash. Then the Coast Guard officer opened the floor to questions from journalists.

"In light of the impressive haul of the operation, will the agencies be increasing their surveillance of boats in the waters between Washington and Vancouver Island?" This question came from a television reporter sporting a stylish but uncomfortable-looking charcoal blazer and matching skirt, once again making Helene grateful radio had no dress code.

"We prefer to give no details of future operations as it might put officers at risk."

Helene was impressed by Jeff's handling of the press conference. He could steer the conversation with as much skill as he manoeuvred a boat. She suspected he would rise through the ranks quickly.

The journalist wasn't surprised when Gary Graham raised his hand to speak. He loved the sound of his own voice too much to miss an opportunity to perform at a press conference.

"And what would you say to the families of those whose loved ones have died from an overdose? Do you expect these kinds of seizures and arrests to bring them any comfort?" From the tone of his question, it would be possible to believe the reporter cared about victims of the ongoing crisis. However, Helene knew the only thing Gary Graham cared about was Gary Graham and his radio ratings. And exploiting a tragedy to gain an audience was his favourite tactic.

"Our sympathies are always with the families of the children, spouses and parents who have been lost." Jeff paused for a moment to let his words sink in before continuing. "I believe that is all the time we have for questions today."

As the other members of the media started to pack up their electronics, Helene reflected on the news of the drug bust. She couldn't help but wonder if Lee had been scouting for smugglers the last time she saw him on the breakwater. But she did still find it hard to believe he could spot anything without at least a pair of binoculars, not unless he had superhuman vision.

Just as Helene was about to slip her notebook into her backpack, she was addressed by a familiar if unsettling voice.

"Helene, do you have a minute?"

The journalist swung around in her chair to see Detective Kalinowski standing in the aisle.

"Sure, just let me pack up and I will meet you in the hall," replied Helene. She didn't want Gary Graham eavesdropping on any conversation between herself and the police officer. That would be too much like a gift.

When Helene joined Kalinowski outside the room, the journalist noted that the detective was wearing the same olive-green multi-pocket vest she had on the first time they met — the evening Helene discovered the body of Lucy Marino.

"I didn't expect to see you here," stated Helene, "it being a maritime operation."

"We like to support our colleagues on the water. All part of the same team." Kalinowski's words sounded hollow, like something she had memorized out of a leadership manual. This caused Helene to wonder about the real reason she was there.

Was the detective keeping an eye on her?

Did she think the journalist was holding back information?

Had Helene only imagined the feeling of trust between them?

"How is your friend Alex?" This time the detective sounded more genuine. "I hope she's recovering okay."

"She's at home now, thanks for asking. Demanding I bring her a steady supply of ice cream and cat food as atonement for my sins. The cat food is for a cat, obviously," stumbled Helene.

"Obviously," said Kalinowski, allowing a fleeting smile.

Standing in the otherwise empty hallway, under the intense gaze of the detective, Helene felt a strong urge to confess to dumpster diving at the home of Lucy Marino's mother. However, she hadn't gone through the documents and photos yet, so she decided to hold off until she had something substantive to share. She knew being charged for trespassing wouldn't do her career in journalism any favours and she wanted to make sure it was worth fessing up. She appeased a sense of guilt by admitting to making a phone call to Professor Neumann.

"It was only to get a few quotes for the bigger story we are doing on the Grayson paintings. All things considered, he was pretty helpful."

"I was curious what you thought of him. When you spoke, did he mention anything about the hate mail?" asked the detective, cocking her head to one side.

"He just said he hadn't sent them. That he was the victim."

"And did you believe him?"

"Oddly, yes. He is a man of questionable morals, but in this case, I think he was innocent, whatever that means."

"Innocent is not a word I would use to describe anyone connected to this case," muttered the detective under her breath. Helene didn't have the nerve to ask if she was included in that assessment. "Everyone likes telling lies — even the dead, apparently."

"Have you figured out who did send the letters?" Helene wasn't expecting the detective to tell her much, but it was worth a try.

"We are analyzing the envelopes for DNA, but I'm not holding out much hope. No one licks their letters these days. Self-adhesive envelopes are not a police officer's friend." Switching topics, the detective asked, "You mentioned the story you are doing about the two paintings that were recently discovered by Marino. I wanted to ask you whether you think they are real or not. I imagine there is a lot of money at stake."

"Honestly, I think the paintings are more important for the attention they will bring to the museum, which I guess makes you right because that will mean more funding. But I don't have the expertise to give an opinion either way. I only know that everyone I've interviewed claims they are authentic." Helene could tell the detective was genuinely interested in her perspective, so she continued. "Professor Neumann talked about the giant Douglas Fir in the forest landscape being a favourite of Grayson's. And she mentions it in a letter to her sister. She also described an unusual friendship with a fisherman in her writing, and I wonder if it's the same figure on the beach in the second painting. I guess there is really no way to know as 130 years ago people weren't constantly snapping selfies."

"Well, if you learn anything else, let me know. I somehow think that a couple of very rare and expensive paintings could provide a strong motive for murder," the detective stated with frankness. "And I wonder who is going to show up on the opening night of the exhibit."

"You'll be there?" Helene didn't mask her surprise.

"Why not? Not many chances to dress up in a city where fashion follows the weather forecast, not the runways."

Helene assumed this meant Kalinowski would not be wearing her olive-green hunting vest to the event.

Knowing she had to get back to the station to file her story on the drug bust, Helene said goodbye to the detective. However, on the way out the door she was accosted by Gary Graham, who seemed to have lain in wait for her.

"You seem awfully cozy with that police detective. Anything you want to share with a colleague?"

Helene turned to face the reporter, believing a direct approach was necessary at this point. "Gary, a colleague is someone who I respect and trust. I can safely say neither is true for you. Now, please, can we go back to happily coexisting while never speaking?" Helene swept past the reporter and didn't look back.

Chapter 18

Helene didn't consider herself a procrastinator. She had never handed in a late paper at university, and her taxes were always done weeks ahead of the deadline. However, she did like to have the time and space to give a task proper attention. So, between putting away piles of badly folded laundry, dropping off new prescriptions for Alex and getting stories on the radio, it took a couple of days before she finally retrieved the bag of documents and photos from the back of a closet. She cleared off the kitchen table to create the space to sort through the items that had been hastily retrieved from the dumpster.

It was the weekend, she had already fed her children lunch, and they were both contently watching shows on their tablets. Helene assumed she wouldn't be disturbed by any demands for the next hour that didn't simply involve giving the children permission to eat sugar of some variation.

She had enjoyed an especially rejuvenating walk along the breakwater in the morning. The colours of the sunrise had created orange and purple stripes on the gentle waves, like a painter had swept a canvas from left to right with a wide brush. Having stretched out her limbs after a week of being curled up in front of a computer keyboard, she now felt physically calm, her mind ready for a fresh diversion.

Helene started by examining the loose papers, some of them ringed with old coffee stains. The first few were nothing more than old estimates for work to be done on the house of the curator's mother. Apparently, the inheritance had come with a leaky roof and a malfunctioning furnace. But she then found a correspondence between the curator and a university in Montreal. It was an offer to be a guest lecturer in September, to speak about the newly discovered works of Amelia Grayson. Perhaps the paintings were going to allow Marino to return to the world of academia after leaving under a cloud so many years ago.

Sooner than she expected, she heard the soft patter of her son's footsteps in the kitchen. He must have finished an episode of his new favourite wildlife cartoon featuring surfing squirrels. The journalist did not even look up from the papers she was reading, expecting to simply hear a request for licorice. Instead, Oscar came to stand next to her at the kitchen table, surveying the mess his mother had made.

Like a heat-seeking missile with a solitary mission, Oscar quickly spotted the only item that could have been of any interest to the ten-year-old boy.

"What's that?" he asked in a soft yet eager voice.

Helene glanced up from the paper she was holding to look where her son was pointing.

"What's what, sweetheart?" But even as she spoke, her eyes located the object of her son's attention: a discount book full of tickets for whale-watching tours was lying in a stack she had yet to sort, with a drawing of an orca fin on the front that had obviously caught Oscar's eye. The journalist hadn't realized the packet had been swept up into her bag when she was filling it in the dumpster. Why a museum curator would have a predilection for whale watching Helene could not imagine. Perhaps it was a way to entertain important donors or artists who visited the museum. Nothing was more stereotypical Victoria than a bumpy two-hour tour in a zodiac boat hunting an endangered species with a camera. It worked up an appetite for partaking of high tea in the style of 19th century British aristocrats, another favoured activity among tourists.

Sitting in her small kitchen, the sun streaming through the window, Helene wondered if it had been a mistake not to tell her children about her fear of riding in boats. She had taken her children on ferries before, but these seemed more like floating buildings than ships. Over the years she had managed to keep her maritime anxiety to herself, mostly because she didn't want to pass it on to Oscar and Cleo. She did the same thing when going to the dentist, pretending it didn't bring back nauseating memories of having teeth pulled by a sadist in the 1970s, a time when parents didn't supervise the professionals who purported to care for their children.

As Helene's heart filled with panic, she watched her son pick up the book of whale-watching tickets and touch the cover with a reverence usually reserved for holy relics or vintage hockey cards.

Peering up at his mother under long eyelashes, Oscar didn't have to say a word. Because of his allergies he had experienced more trauma than most children his age, and even during a simple school lunch he had to guard against being touched by a classmate eating bananas or dairy. So when it came to refusing her son a chance to witness the animal which dominated his drawings and dreams, Helene knew she didn't have the strength. Especially when she found herself in possession of half a dozen tickets which usually cost hundreds of dollars each.

She wasn't entirely clear on the ethics of taking something valuable from a dumpster, but the joy on her son's face when she agreed to the ocean journey vanquished any moral misgivings. Embracing her delighted child before he went back to his shows, Helene tried to ignore visions of hungry waves lapping over the gunwale of a narrow boat.

Thinking that waiting a whole week for the ocean voyage would only let the dread build up, Helene decided she would take her children on the whale-watching tour the next day. For once the sun was making an appearance on the weekend, so she figured she might as well take advantage of it. However, Helene could no longer concentrate on the documents that were strewn across the kitchen table, not to mention it felt a bit too much like doing work on a Saturday, so she packed everything back into the grocery bag and returned it to the closet.

After unloading the dishwasher, she lay down on the couch and indulged in a few episodes of a historical drama set in Edwardian England. But the vapid liaisons of the upper classes couldn't hold her attention, not to mention the fact that women were only appreciated for their ornamental value. Was this the world Amelia Grayson rejected by remaining an unmarried painter? If so, Helene could completely empathize with her life choices.

As morning turned to afternoon, apprehension for the whale-watching tour continued to lurk in the back of Helene's mind, like an ocean predator swimming just below the surface. The journalist decided the only way to shake off the sense of foreboding was to engage with her children. She took her son on a walk through Beacon Hill Park, during which his indefatigable imagination transformed ordinary trees and rocks into powerful spaceships and priceless gems. Her sole responsibility on the outdoor adventure was to store the pinecones and sticks he gathered along the way. Her coat pockets were lumpy and heavy by the time they returned home, but her heart was much lighter.

In the evening, Helene invited her children to pick a movie they could all watch together in her bedroom. Now that her daughter was a teenager, and her son still ten, it was no longer easy to find a show that appealed to both of them. He enjoyed cartoons featuring raccoons riding motorcycles while his sister had lately been bingeing on '80s sitcoms. They ended up putting on the original *Star Wars* movie, which they had seen so many times that her two children could recite the dialogue of both the heroic and villainous space-dwelling characters while they battled for dominion over the galaxy. This, however, resulted in Helene spending a restless night dreaming about Imperial sharks whose fins glowed like lightsabres.

The morning rush of packing clothing, allergy medication and snacks for the whale-watching expedition kept Helene's anxiety over the trip at low tide, but once they were down at the dock waiting to board the vessel, her fears came rushing in like a tsunami. And like all of the imagined catastrophes that played out in her mind, these terrors included threats to the safety of her children. Visions of a capsized boat and a scramble for life jackets made her cringe while the tour guide went through a short safety demonstration. She was holding Oscar's hand and had probably been squeezing it too hard as he looked up at her with concerned eyes. Like any parent in this situation, she tried to adopt a confident smile, but her son didn't look convinced. The child shuffled a little closer to his mother as though it was his job to bring her comfort, not the other way around.

Stepping onto the zodiac was an act of sheer will for Helene. It didn't help that the vessel was inflatable rather than made of more solid material. Had it been composed of wood, she thought, at least you could cling to a plank if it came apart in a storm. The passengers had all put on awkward life vests, but the journalist knew the cold of the water could kill you almost as fast as drowning. Tragic scenes from movies featuring maritime disasters played through her mind as she settled into one corner of the vessel.

Once all the passengers were on board, the tour guide started up the noisy engine, and the group raced across the harbour. At this point, Helene could at least appreciate the view from the perspective of a photographer. An infinite spectrum of blues was corralled by the boundary of the ocean's horizon while the clouds silently but restlessly evolved into supple shapes. The boat was enveloped in the vast expanse of the water and sky, almost a different galaxy with its own laws of movement and gravity. And although fear was still a churning knot in her stomach, all the other worries of everyday life shrank away like the land in the distance.

The journalist was also pleased to see Cleo using her cell phone to take pictures of the scenery. Her daughter's growing passion for photography was one way Helene felt she could connect with the teenager. The motor of the boat was too loud for conversation, so Cleo simply leaned over to share one of the shots she had captured. Helene smiled and gave her daughter a thumbs up. Glancing over at her son, she saw he looked as delighted as any ten-year-old boy flying over waves would be.

The rocky shores of Vancouver Island were to the left of the boat as they journeyed along the water to the area where the southern resident killer whales were known to swim. Helene did her best to keep her eyes up, either on the bordering land or the water in front, because when she did accidentally glance down, a wave of nausea was her reward. She desperately didn't want to ruin this day for her son by becoming overwhelmed by her fear of travel by water.

She couldn't recall exactly what caused her nautical terrors since there hadn't been one specific traumatic incident that had changed her relationship with boats. As a teenager, she had taken canoeing lessons at a summer camp, and she recalled a sense of serenity as she broke through the surface of the water with each stroke. However, there were also paddle boats at the facility, and sometimes the submerged crank shaft would get caught in the reeds if she travelled too close to the shore. To get free, Helene would have to swim under the boat and rip the tangle of slippery grasses from the gears. It didn't take much imagination to transform the swaying motion of the stalks into the slither of malevolent underwater creatures. But it wasn't until years later that Helene found herself actively turning down a chance to go for a day trip on a catamaran in Mexico. Maybe her fear had simply been growing inside her over time, gaining strength from seemingly trivial negative experiences. And then one day, with the right trigger, the terror arrived fully formed like a sort of emotional black butterfly from a toxic cocoon.

The zodiac had been bouncing over the ocean for almost forty-five minutes and Helene was starting to wonder if they would manage to track down the aquatic mammals that day. *Surely there must be some trips when the tourists come back disappointed*, she speculated. But then the vessel rounded a corner of the rocky coastline and there was a cluster of telltale fins about half a kilometre directly ahead of them. The pilot immediately killed the engines as maritime regulations didn't allow vessels to get too close to the orcas.

Oscar had brought his prized binoculars on the trip, and he leaned against the inflated side of the boat, rapidly focusing the lenses. Cleo removed her cell phone from a waterproof bag again and zoomed in on the creatures to take dozens of shots. For Helene, the fluid movements of the black-and-white ocean-dwellers were breathtaking. However, what truly warmed her heart were the excited exchanges between her son and daughter, their age and maturity gap overcome by the thrill of witnessing the southern resident killer whales splash and tumble in the waves. A gasp went up among the tour group when one of the orcas leaped out of the water, its massive body gracefully arcing in the air. Cleo managed to capture a stunning photo of the creature, showing the image first to her brother and then to her mother with pride. While the other passengers exchanged jubilant chatter, Helene was grateful she hadn't let her fear get in the way of having such an incredible experience with her family.

The zodiac remained a safe distance from the orcas while the tour group continued to observe and take photos.

At the same time, Helene caught sight of another boat travelling at speed through the ocean passage.

The fast-moving vessel looked like a fishing boat, the kind wealthy Americans might rent for a day excursion. Perhaps an excuse to drink beer more than to actually bring home any kind of dripping trophy in need of scaling.

Out of curiosity, Helene asked Oscar if she could borrow his binoculars, which he gave up with slight reluctance. Holding them up, it took a moment to find the boat through the eye pieces. But after finally managing to focus on her quarry, she was shocked to recognize Jeff at the helm of the boat. And standing on the deck, staring back at the wake of the vessel, was Lee in his wool cap.

Helene had a sudden urge to wave at the Coast Guard officer, but something about the urgency of the speed of the boat and the serious set of Lee's features stopped her from lifting an arm. She wouldn't want to interfere with a smuggling investigation like the one shared at the press conference the previous day. She was curious to register a note of sadness at missing an encounter with Lee once more. But then the squeals of her delighted son and daughter brought her back to her own boat, as the orcas seemed inclined to perform for the group that day — perhaps the creatures were inspired by the generous laughter of children.

March 30, 1886

My dearest Constance,

    I am so pleased to receive the news that your excursion to the Lake District has eased the complaints in your chest, and I am hoping your good health remains. I have immensely enjoyed the delightful recounting of your daily jaunts and am quite confident I could paint a faithful landscape of the mercurial sky and boundless hills. The sketches of the shoreline by young Ernest could have been done by the French impressionist Monet, he gives the water such a sense of movement it almost dances off the page. I wonder if I shouldn't send you funds to purchase an easel for his approaching birthday.

    In these recent weeks, I do myself possess an abundance of inspiration. Perhaps the success of the exhibition has given me renewed faith in my abilities. But more likely it is simply the resplendent floral bounty of spring with which I am surrounded. Such beauty awaits me the moment I step off the wooden threshold of my house, almost making an entreaty to be painted.

    It has become my habit to take a walk along the rocky beaches at dawn where I will often encounter my fisherman. Apparently, if you wish to catch a creature of the sea, fish or human, you must wake with the sun!

    Two days past, in the early light, Charlie was making repairs to his net, a task that takes much skill and deftness of hand. He took a moment of repose from his labour and made me the boldest of offers, a tour of the harbour in his vessel. I know this is a proposal you will consider most shocking. And yet I did heartily agree to the adventure!

It is in fact true that I have not travelled by water since my arrival from England more than a decade ago. After the tiresome ocean voyage, I had endured enough swaying and rocking to make me most appreciative of the fixedness of dry land. I have come to perceive the ocean as a subject for a painting, not a place of exploration. But once I was in Charlie's bobbing vessel, the land having slipped away, I felt such freedom, only to be compared to when my mind is in an ecstasy of creativity and daily concerns cannot touch me. I have to admit that at one moment I also felt I had come to dwell in one of my own paintings.

I must tell you, dear sister, I feel a momentous shift happening in my life. At present I cannot yet find the words to commit it to paper, and if I were so bold, I fear it would give you an even greater shock than my nautical ventures.

And now I have the excuse of a visitor to draw this letter to a close. Margaret has just arrived for afternoon tea. Her company has not become any more amiable of late, but I cannot find a way to make an end to our friendship. Oh, to be done with the politeness of society and live an honest life, like a fisherman earning his keep from the sea.

I promise to soon muster the courage to share the new notions tugging at my heart like a strong moon tide. For now, I send kisses across the seas, to you and the darling children.

With steadfast affection,

   Amelia

Chapter 19

Helene did not appreciate a cliffhanger, especially not in the last episode of a streaming show that hadn't been renewed for another season, and certainly not at the end of a letter written in 1886. To make matters worse, this was the last of the correspondence included in the pamphlet she had taken from the museum, leaving her feeling both frustrated and cheated.

Tossing the booklet of Victorian writing on the kitchen table next to her bowl of granola, the journalist let out an exasperated sigh. Not only was she frustrated by the lack of answers surrounding the death of Lucy Marino, but she was also piqued by the mystery surrounding Amelia Grayson in the weeks before her disappearance a hundred years ago.

What was the artist's new direction?
Was she talking about her art or her life?
What came of her connection to the fisherman?

It seemed like a very unconventional friendship for the era, a female painter born to the upper classes, and a man who had probably never set foot in a formal drawing room.

Helene had extra time to consider the mysteries surrounding the letter because her morning was a little less hectic than usual. Her kids were on spring break, which meant she didn't have to pack lunches or drive them to school. Oscar and Cleo decided not to go to any day camps that March — they were just going to entertain themselves at home while Helene was at work. The journalist had bought some high-quality art paper in the hopes they might use the paints she retrieved from the dumpster. She was determined they wouldn't spend their whole vacation on tablets.

The break from the morning school routine also left Helene enough time to make a short stop on the way into the newsroom. She decided to try to get to the bottom of one mystery, even if it was more than a century old.

A half hour later she was knocking on the front door of the Amelia Grayson Museum, wondering if any of the staff would be in before 9:00 AM. Thankfully she soon heard the sound of a deadbolt being slid open, which was followed by a greeting from the confused-looking archivist.

"Good morning, Hana," said Helene brightly. "Do you have a few moments to spare? I have a couple of questions I was hoping someone could answer."

The archivist let Helene into the building, albeit in a slightly begrudging manner. Maybe she just wasn't a morning person. The two women did not speak again until they were settled on either side of the desk in Hana's office. The journalist had turned down an offer of tea, wanting to get to the matter at hand right away.

"Do you have more questions about the exhibit for the two paintings that opens on Thursday? I was sure we had gone over everything," the archivist asked, not bothering to hide a note of impatience.

"No, that's all set. I will just add a few quotes and photos from the evening of the unveiling, and then we will publish the piece. I think it's going to get a lot of attention. Thanks again for your help."

"My pleasure."

"I'm here for a different reason. The first time I came to visit you, I spotted a box of pamphlets containing letters by Grayson to her sister in England. They have given me real insight into her life and what she was up against as a female artist during those times."

"Where did you find the pamphlets?" the archivist asked in a tone that sounded friendly but really wasn't. Helene decided to avoid answering the question entirely, since it was hardly the point.

"I finally finished reading the letters written by Amelia, and she obviously had a close relationship with her sister despite the distance between them. And such a style of writing! It certainly was a more poetic time."

"Yes, well, we decided not to sell the pamphlets in the end. They are a small snapshot of her life, so things could be taken out of context."

Helene was once again impressed by the archivist's commitment to protecting the legacy of Grayson. She probably didn't want the mystery raised in the last letter to be the target of speculation. But that didn't stop Helene from hunting for answers.

"I can't help wondering about where the missing letters are, and I was hoping you might have them."

"Missing letters?"

"Yes. You see, she wrote a letter once every two weeks, quite faithfully, during those spring months. The last one was from March 30th, 1886, and I know Amelia wasn't declared missing until the end of May. That means she must have written at least one if not two more letters to her sister."

"Can I ask what this has to do with the opening of the exhibit?" The archivist was looking over the rim of her glasses in a slightly disapproving way.

Helene was taken aback. She considered the mystery of the missing letters worth exploring for its own sake. But, to be fair, the upcoming opening exhibit meant the archivist probably had more pressing issues.

"My apologies. I'm sure you're very busy right now. It's just that I finished the collection last night, and I'm a journalist — I don't like loose ends." Helene paused for a moment before trying to articulate her thoughts more clearly. "And yet, don't you think it's possible some clues to the mystery of Grayson's disappearance might be contained in the last letters she wrote?"

"I don't see why they would be. And honestly, as you said, I am very busy. And I don't really want to dredge up the debate around Grayson's disappearance right now. The focus needs to be on her incredible legacy. A woman defying the norms of the time. Rejecting marriage and even romance for the sake of art."

It was clear the archivist wanted her visitor to leave, which of course made Helene want to do the opposite. "Can you just tell me if anyone knows what might have happened to the rest of the letters?"

The archivist must have realized Helene needed some kind of information to appease her curiosity. She reluctantly replied, "My understanding is that there was a fire at the home of her sister In England. Some of the letters and possibly a few drawings Grayson had sent from Canada were lost. But so much time has passed. It's hard to know what really happened."

Helene experienced a cooling flush of disappointment. The archivist was right. A fire on the other side of the Atlantic, more than a hundred years ago, was not likely to give up its secrets now. The journalist knew she was beaten and that it was time to get to work. Rising property taxes in Victoria and a petition for a new dog park in Saanich were what she should be focusing on.

When she arrived at the office only a few minutes late, the first thing Helene did was open her email. At the top of her inbox was a message from Alex.

Good morning, H.

Just wanted to let you know I really appreciate you taking care of me last week. As a happily single woman, it is good to know I will not starve to death on the couch when I get sick or forget how to order takeout. They say marriage is in sickness and in health, but clearly our friendship extends to poisoning by chocolate, so that seems even better. Or perhaps we are more like sisters than a married couple, a bit of healthy sibling rivalry, but there is no one I would rather get drunk with. Anyway, I don't think anyone says thank you enough anymore, so I am saying thank you.

By the way, can you bring me some more mangos? I didn't know fruit could taste like that. Like Mexico in a bowl. Really annoying peel, though.

Oh yes, Daisy says hi and that she really prefers the high-end cat food.

Your friend,

A.

Before getting to work on a radio story about the closure of a popular coffee shop in Esquimalt due to a condo development, Helene printed up the email from Alex and pinned it to the board over her desk next to her son's latest drawing of an orca arcing through the air. She knew it was important to hold onto mementoes from people you cared about. At times life could drown you in troubles, and a reminder that you mattered to someone could be a raft to cling to in a storm.

She supposed the sister of Amelia Grayson had kept a tidy package of the correspondence from Canada tied up with a ribbon in a Victorian hat box, which really didn't explain how only some of the letters were burned in a fire. But if Alex was going to call her a kind of sister, Helene was just grateful they didn't have a relationship like Lucy and Paola Marino, with the surviving sister so impatient to consign the other's legacy to a dumpster.

Shaking off thoughts of complicated relationships, Helene was determined to focus her attention on the story about the coffee shop. It had been opened by the grandfather of the current owner, Dimitri Yakupov, in the 1960s. Helene imagined the family came to Vancouver Island as Russian émigrés at a time when it was still largely dominated by British culture. Not to mention the Cold War was very hot in that decade, and there must have been some prejudice against anyone sounding like a James Bond villain. She wondered if the senior Yakupov was still alive and up for an interview.

By making a quick phone call, Helene arranged to meet both the grandson and grandfather at the coffee shop in the afternoon. This would give her a chance to take some photos of the café, which had hockey memorabilia from the 1970s that depicted the rivalry between Canadian and Russian teams on its walls. The journalist hoped she would be able to interview a few customers about the closure of the iconic café as well.

Helene knew that having the voice of the elder Yakupov in her coffee shop story would give it more depth and context. And this got her thinking about the coverage of the Grayson paintings again. The unmarried artist had no children of her own by the time she disappeared, but maybe the journalist could reach out to the descendants of her sister Constance — Grayson's letters did mention a niece and a nephew. Wouldn't it be incredible to have the reaction of Grayson's living relations to the newly discovered paintings?

It was probably safe to assume the archivist had contacts for family in England, tucked away in a forgotten folder somewhere. However, Helene didn't want to bother Hana twice in one day, figuring she had used up her quota of patience with her questions about the missing letters.

Helene had several hours before heading to the café in Esquimalt, so she did an online search for any records of Grayson's family. What she soon discovered was that the painter's nephew had gone on to become an artist himself.

The journalist smiled at the thought that Amelia's praise for the early drawings of her sister's son might have influenced his path in life.

Constance's son, Ernest Bailey, had started off his career by doing political cartoons for newspapers at the beginning of the 20th century, covering movements such as Irish Home Rule and the suffragettes. However, when the First World War broke out, he accompanied troops to the front lines. In the early years, he sent back patriotic pictures of brave soldiers battling the enemy, metal bayonets glinting in the sun. But by the time he returned to the shores of England, he was producing graphic oil paintings that revealed the true horrors of trench warfare. His most famous work was of a broken man in a bloodied uniform holding the corpse of his fallen comrade.

The rawness of Bailey's work made him fall out of public favour, and it took several decades for the artist to be lauded for the honesty of the discomforting reality he had depicted. Like his Canadian aunt, he also died with no known children, but his sister, Minnie, had gone on to become the guardian of his legacy. This mantle had been passed down through the generations, and recently her great-great-granddaughter had created a website dedicated to Ernest Bailey.

Copying the email address from the website, Helene sent a short query asking about the possibility of a phone interview. She mentioned the upcoming exhibition of the two paintings by her ancestor Amelia Grayson and the fact that the event was receiving national attention.

The journalist did some quick calculations of the eight-hour time difference between Victoria, BC and Leeds in Yorkshire, where she garnered that Sybil Bancroft, the relative of the two famous painters, now lived. She proposed calling when it was morning on the west coast of Canada and evening in Great Britain. Before pressing send on the email, she couldn't help but add a few lines asking about the mystery of the artist's missing letters. After all, what harm could it do?

Helene was preparing to run across the street to grab a sandwich before heading out to the café in Esquimalt when her desk phone rang. Like most of her fellow journalists, she had almost completely stopped using the office phone years ago, her cell being the one number at which she was always reachable. Besides being an incredibly undependable way for people to reach her, the work phone was also the line unhappy radio listeners called to complain about the station's particular coverage of a story. The reporters were regularly accused of being a left-wing mouthpiece for Victoria City Council. If that wasn't bad enough, lonely conspiracy theorists often dialled up to share their thoughts on sunsets containing coded messages from aliens or, even worse, communists. Understandably, the journalist usually ignored the phone like the crying of some anachronistic device that didn't know when to die. But for some reason, on this occasion, even though her stomach was growling with impatience, she picked up the receiver.

"Hello, Vancouver Island Radio, Helene Unger speaking."

"Is that Helene? Oh, I'm so glad I reached you. I wasn't sure if this was your direct line."

The journalist was already kicking herself for answering the call. This person sounded quite desperate.

"Can I ask who's calling?" Helene sighed in expectation of a long and convoluted conversation. She put her backpack on her desk and sat down in her chair again.

"You probably don't remember me. My name is Paola, Paola Marino. You came to my bakery to talk about my sister Lucy."

All thoughts of food forgotten, Helene connected the voice with the name of the caller.

"Paola, of course, how can I help?"

155

"Well, you seemed so curious about my sister when we met. What I mean is, you seemed like a decent person. Interested in the truth, anyway. So now I'm hoping you can help me."

"What's happened?" Helene asked with trepidation.

"The police have asked me to come in for more questioning. I think they think I might have killed my sister."

"Why would they?" asked Helene, curious how much Paola would reveal.

"Well, I guess the fact that I am probably going to inherit a house from my sister. I am her closest relative, even though we weren't close at all."

"Your relationship was a bit acrimonious."

"That doesn't mean I killed her. And that's why I need your help. You've got to prove that I didn't do it. Isn't the point of journalists — to stop the wrong people from going to jail?"

Helene had never heard her job described like that, but she supposed trying to make sure the right person was arrested for the murder of Lucy Marino boiled down to just about the same thing.

Before hanging up the phone, Helene promised Paola she would continue investigating Lucy's death. The plaintive and grateful words of the otherwise gruff baker was a powerful reminder to the journalist that her work could alter the lives of others. The weight of the situation made her long for the days she worked in a bowling alley, when she was merely responsible for untangling fallen pins, not solving a murder plot.

Chapter 20

When Helene interviewed individuals for a social justice story, they usually fell into one of two categories: they were either the person being oppressed, or the one doing the oppressing. It was very clear-cut in cases of prejudice and racism — a doctor who had refused proper medical care to an Indigenous Elder, a student excluded from a school committee because of their sexual orientation. In other kinds of reporting there was also usually a victim, but sometimes the harm was being done by something bigger than a person, like climate change or disability rates below the poverty line. But no matter the circumstances, there usually wasn't ambivalence about whether someone was a culprit or a casualty. However, it seemed that Paola Marino may have shifted from one camp to another.

Helene's first suspect in the murder of Lucy Marino was her sister. The lucrative inheritance and the lifelong animosity were impossible to ignore. The fact that Paola appeared untouched by grief did not put her in a great light either. But would a guilty person call up a reporter and implore them to prove their innocence? Especially when that same journalist had just done a story celebrating the life of the sibling they were under suspicion of murdering. The one thing Helene knew for certain was that she had to find a way to figure out the identity of the killer, even if it meant discovering that the sister who claimed to be innocent was in fact guilty. But before any of that, Helene first had to do an interview about the death of a café.

Dimitri Yakupov welcomed her to his coffee shop with open arms and a triple-cheek kiss, which was the custom in some European countries. As a member of the media,

Helene was used to people being slightly more nervous or even suspicious when they first met her, but Dimitri radiated warmth. In fact, it was the journalist who was a bit intimidated by their initial encounter as the Russian had the barrel chest and looming height of a hockey enforcer. The café owner refused to even consider starting the interview until she had sampled a plate of sweet rugelach dusted with icing sugar. Helene made enthusiastic noises while munching on the Russian treat, which seemed to please Dimitri to no end.

Once her empty plate had been cleared away, he brought out a cup of coffee for Helene. Then he returned once more to the kitchen, this time to accompany his grandfather to the table where the journalist was sitting with her recording equipment. Dimitri explained that as his grandfather was almost ninety, he had reverted to mostly communicating only in Russian. He offered to translate Helene's questions for the interview.

What followed was the kind of experience Helene cherished most as a journalist, when a reporter had the privilege to bear witness to a story that captured the resiliency of the human spirit.

Dimitri's grandfather, Vasili, had been a professor of literature in the Soviet Union in the early 1960s. He had a good position and a big apartment in the centre of Moscow. However, as some of his colleagues started to speak out about banned books and censorship of information, Vasili could not remain silent. The professor started going on protest marches, and he even penned a few letters in dissident newspapers before they too were banned.

One night, when Dimitri's grandmother was pregnant with his father, a neighbour knocked on the door to warn them that the police were on their way. It seemed Vasili's activities had caught the attention of the authorities, and they wanted to make an example of him. The couple bundled a few possessions into a leather suitcase and boarded a train to Vyborg. Thankfully, the professor had a brother who lived in the historic border town near Finland. Eventually his grandparents managed to not only escape from the Soviet Union but also to elude detection by Finnish officials, who sometimes sent back defectors to likely languish or die in labour camps.

When the couple finally made their way to Canada, there was no hope of Vasili finding a position at a university — he simply didn't have the fluency in English. Instead, they decided to open a small café in the community of Esquimalt, serving Turkish coffee alongside Russian delicacies. Each of their four children spent time working in the coffee shop as they grew up, but eventually it was his grandson Dimitri who took over when Vasili retired. And yet, almost ten years since handing over the keys, the elder Yakupov could still be found puttering in the café's kitchen on most days.

Dimitri translated for his grandfather, who was becoming increasingly agitated, explaining that after escaping the terrors of the Soviet Union and building a new life from scratch in Canada, he was going to watch his legacy be destroyed by developers. The building the café had occupied for more than fifty years was to be torn down and replaced by high-end condominiums. Promises had been made to the family about being allowed to rent space in the new construction, but the rates were prohibitive. Dimitri remained hopeful of finding a different home for the café, but Helene could see the light had gone out of Vasili's eyes. He didn't have the energy for another battle in this lifetime. Real estate developers had extinguished a spirit that had survived the KGB.

Once she had finished interviewing the two men, Helene managed to speak to a few customers who shared their disappointment and frustration at losing the café. It was a community gathering spot that held music and poetry nights, an antidote to a world where most people streamed shows from the isolation of their homes. Helene felt a twinge of guilt at this last comment, as exhaustion usually kept her from making any plans after work. She told herself that maybe once her kids were older, she could start attending arts events again. At least she went for a walk on the breakwater most evenings.

Helene left the café with the makings of a heartfelt story of triumph and loss along with a small box of sugary Russian delicacies. She wasn't supposed to accept gifts from people she interviewed, but the journalist knew her colleagues would appreciate her flexible ethics once they took their first bite of honey cake.

It only took about an hour to put together the story on the café closure, and filing the script and recordings gave Helene a sense of satisfaction she hadn't experienced in quite a while. Unlike when she covered new maritime safety rules or even city council meetings, the piece had sympathetic characters facing simple but daunting challenges. The story was as rich with humanity as the Russian honey cake was replete with sweetness. *Who knows*, she thought, *maybe someone listening to the piece will know of a place where the family could re-establish their café*. It was the hope of most journalists that their work could be the impetus for finding a solution. However, after leaving the office, Helene now had to focus on unravelling a much more complicated story. And she knew where to start searching for answers again.

When she arrived home, the journalist had to clean up her children's lunch leftovers and then cook dinner for everyone. The day after the whale-watching trip, both Oscar and Cleo radiated a calm contentment — the watery adventure had clearly given them a much-needed distraction from the rhythm of their usual routines.

It wasn't until just after 7:00 when Helene finally retrieved the battered grocery bag from the back of the closet once more. But this time, after dumping the contents on the kitchen table, she skipped trying to methodically sort through every paper she had collected from the sister's dumpster and went straight for the oversized envelope of photographs. If a picture was worth a thousand words, then maybe one of those words was a clue that would help solve a murder.

First checking over her shoulder to make sure Cleo and Oscar weren't in the room, in case the images were inappropriate for children, Helene then placed the short stack of photos in front of her on the table. The first shot she examined was of a much younger-looking version of Lucy Marino. She had lush hair and a youthful smile, and she looked hopeful and a bit mischievous. When compared to the photo Helene had accidentally taken of Marino at the breakwater a few months ago, it appeared the past ten years had transformed the woman's countenance to one of stubborn determination.

Helene flipped through a few more photos that seemed to be from the same era. Several revealed a studio full of young painters sitting in front of easels, which suggested to Helene that they must have been taken while Marino was at college. But then she came to an image that made her freeze and check again that her children weren't nearby.

The photo was taken from behind, capturing an older man holding a woman around the waist. Both were wearing no clothing. The dark-haired male was nibbling on the ear of the female who was facing away from the camera. The only distinguishing detail of the obscured figure was an upper-arm tattoo of purple lilacs, an interesting alternative from the ever-popular rose. Helene was easily able to identify the older man as Professor Neumann, and she felt a shiver of disgust at the predatory set of his features in the throes of what was obviously a sexual conquest.

The photo was taken low down, at an odd angle and in very poor light, which made Helene doubt whether the subjects had given their consent. And then, of course, the

161

journalist had to think of a justification for why Lucy Marino, a museum curator, would have an intimate photo of a professor and another woman in her possession. After she couldn't come up with a good reason, that just left a bad one — blackmail.

Had Lucy threatened her former professor with the photos?

And who was the mystery woman?

Was this image a motive for murder?

Helene's first instinct was to pick up the phone and call Detective Kalinowski. There was no doubt this compromising photo found among Marino's possessions would put renewed focus on Professor Neumann as a suspect, but the journalist had already made one mistake when it came to investigating the academic: upon discovering the pile of hate mail in his office drawer, she had assumed he was the culprit when it turned out he was a victim too. So, Helene wanted to make sure she had the facts straight before sending the police after the academic again.

Helene decided she would try to speak to one of Lucy's former classmates once more, although the florist Benjamin Cornish was certainly out of the question as he had lied about even knowing the curator. But the artist Rosa Winter had been quite helpful when it came to remembering details about the other students at art college. She was also one of the few people connected with the murder investigation who seemed to be content in life. Helene reflected on whether this was because she was the only one to follow through on her dream of becoming an artist. Despite the fact that Benjamin Cornish had made a fortune selling bouquets of flowers, his persona as a bon vivant came off as slightly wilted. And Lucy Marino appeared to live without affection from friends or family, hardly the mark of a well-curated existence.

162

Taking stock of her own life choices — becoming a journalist and a mother — Helene considered herself to be happy. It was true that most of the time she was exhausted, rushing from home to school to work and then trying to squeeze in a trip to the grocery store for more bacon. Admittedly, sometimes, after a weekend of cleaning grubby bathrooms and a greasy stove, she would longingly recall the year she spent in Prague, in her late twenties. Memories of stumbling over the cobblestones of Václavské Náměstí, a plastic cup of mulled wine in hand, seemed so foreign to her current middle-aged existence. But then she would recall the loneliness of a crowded tram of people speaking an unfamiliar language. Even youth hostels lacked the romance of the tales found in travel guides, of nomadic youth gathered around wooden tables, sharing crusty bread and stories of cheap train rides to castles. Instead, she ended up eating her cold dinner in a cramped room to avoid leering men and their offers of a private tour of the historic Charles Bridge.

As if she could sense her mother needed rescuing from despondent recollections, Cleo walked into the kitchen and opened the refrigerator door. The teenager gazed into the white light of the humming appliance as though it held the mystery of existence or at least the ultimate combination of sweet and salty food. Grabbing the last slice of a nut-free carrot cake with delight, Cleo didn't even look at Helene before exiting the room, also omitting to take a fork from the drawer since she generally considered utensils to be optional. However, under her breath, the journalist's daughter distinctly mumbled the words "love you." And the surge of joy it sparked in Helene made her confident she had made a few good choices in life — at least when it came to her career, children and carrot cake.

Chapter 21

School buildings from a certain era had a very particular smell, with walls the colour of weak tea absorbing the sweat of young bodies over decades. Helene only had to walk through the front entrance of the local James Bay Community School to be transported back to her own elementary education experience in Windsor Park, Edmonton. Thankfully, this structure did not also have separate entrances for boys and girls, like the school of her childhood, an enforcement of prescriptive gender roles from a bygone era. But otherwise, the children's art on the walls was as timeless as the lost-and-found box, a metaphor for the human condition if there ever was one.

The public exhibition for Amelia Grayson's paintings was just two nights away, and Helene could feel her anticipation growing. She believed it wasn't only the paintings that would be revealed at the event, but some important clue to the murder of the curator. The journalist couldn't explain why she had this conviction, but it simply felt like everything was leading up to the evening. Attending a community craft and art sale on a Tuesday after work seemed to be part of a natural progression culminating in the Grayson exhibition.

When she had decided to speak to Rosa Winter again about Lucy Marino and her other former classmates, Helene had returned to the artist's website. There was a notice on the page that the painter was going to take part in a fair at the neighbourhood elementary school. She decided to show up in person rather than making a phone call. There was no other way to share the photograph, as sending an intimate

164

picture in a text message without consent was illegal as well as unethical.

As she made her way into the main gymnasium on the Tuesday evening, it was buzzing with the voices of eager vendors. There were about thirty rented tables in the room, displaying everything from cutting boards crafted from oak to hand-knit stuffies for children. Helene knew that shopping at a fair like this was not only a way to support local artisans but also a statement against the globalization of the economy. But Helene acknowledged it was an uphill battle, with grandma's crochet octopuses up against the latest movie marketing machine promoting plastic figurines mass produced in Bangladesh. And unlike in the movies, when it came to commercial competition, the underdog, or under-octopus, did not usually win.

Helene spotted Rosa Winter in the corner of the room surrounded by a dozen of her bright paintings on display easels. The artist was wearing a simple navy blue boatneck sweater with checked capri pants and flat shoes, a style reminiscent of Audrey Hepburn. Her hair was cut in a short straight bob, and unlike most other female artists Helene had encountered, it was not accessorized by a flowing floral scarf.

The journalist had previously looked at Winter's art online, but the brilliant colours of her stylized scenes of Victoria were even more intense in real life. Helene was immediately drawn to a painting of the breakwater at sunset that could have been inspired by one of the many photographs she had taken on her regular walks. The concrete promenade seemed to be floating above the water, giving it a slightly surreal aspect, a right angle cutting across the flowing lines of simplified waves. The sky was illuminated by thick coloured streaks of sunset. The journalist was grateful the price tag for the piece was hidden as she could already imagine it hanging over her mantlepiece. With the cost of Cleo's orthodontic work

165

clouding her financial future, the last thing she needed to be doing was calculating whether she could afford a painting.

"It's one of my favourite places to paint." The artist had come around the table to approach Helene on the right.

"I go there almost every day," Helene replied, eyes still fixed on the painting. "A kind of pilgrimage that keeps me from taking a hammer to the dishwasher."

"You must be a parent."

"A single parent."

"Wow. You need art and beautiful things more than anyone." This might have come off as a sales pitch from someone else, but the painter spoke with simple sincerity and concern. "I'm surprised you have time to come out to this craft sale."

"Well, in fact, I don't. But I have an ulterior motive. My name is Helene Unger. We talked before on the phone." She turned to face the artist as she spoke.

"Ah, the journalist — writing about Lucy Marino, if I remember correctly." The artist smiled while responding, clearly not threatened by Helene coming to meet her in person without calling first.

"You were really helpful the last time we spoke," said Helene. "I have a few more questions. And a photo for you to look at."

"A photo? That does sound intriguing." Winter adjusted a painting on an easel as she replied. "Just give me about twenty minutes to finish setting up my table. There was a lady interested in a painting of the Empress Hotel, and I think she was going to come right at the start of the fair."

While waiting for the artist to have time for a private conversation, Helene took the opportunity to check out the wares of the other vendors in the room. As it happened, an island company that sold locally produced beef jerky was at the fair. Their dried meat was a favourite of Oscar's, so she picked up a dozen of the shrink-wrapped packages for his school lunches. Even if she didn't get any new information from Winter that evening about the explicit photograph, at least she wasn't leaving empty-handed.

Walking past the tables of the other vendors, her backpack now weighed down with well-seasoned beef jerky, she wondered about the challenge of being a creative person who needed to be a hustler as well — someone who could not only carve and paint a garden gnome but also hawk it like a newspaper seller. She imagined this was a bit of a stretch for the truly artistic soul. An image of Van Gogh as a used car salesman came to mind. She wondered how much Amelia Grayson worried about selling her paintings. According to her letters, she did experience both critical and financial success. But Grayson had possessed a sizable inheritance that allowed her to walk away from an unappealing marriage and set herself up as an artist.

Once Helene had completed a circuit of the gymnasium, she returned to Winter's table where the artist was wrapping up a painting for a customer. An older woman looked pleased as she walked away with the package under her arm.

"I'm glad you made a sale," said Helene, although relieved to see that the breakwater painting remained on an easel.

The artist shrugged and stated, "I want to sell them and I don't. The whole point of painting is to share my way of seeing things with others. But each piece carries a slice of myself. Selling them is like giving away a fragment of my soul. Which makes me, in some ways, the architect of my own heartbreak." The artist stood silent for a few seconds more and then brightened. "Sorry, I've always had a tendency for the dramatic."

The artist's next words brought Helene's thoughts back to the matter at hand.

"What was it you wanted to talk about? Oh right. Lucy Marino. You mentioned a photograph?"

"I wanted to ask you a few questions first. About Lucy and Professor Neumann. I know he had a bit of a reputation at the art school, among the female students."

"You mean he slept with them?" Winter asked directly.

"Yes, that's what I heard. And I'm wondering if you think he and Lucy had an affair."

"It's funny you should ask that because I think *she* certainly tried to seduce *him*. When things started to go badly at art school, she began to flirt relentlessly with Neumann. Bringing him coffee at the start of class, asking about private office hours. It became almost embarrassing to watch. My suspicion is that she was hoping he could save her from a downward spiral. Yet, despite his reputation, I don't think she ever succeeded with him. Then, after the summer break, she didn't return. No one was surprised. Under the pressure to find her own vision, she seemed to lose all confidence."

Helene was surprised to hear that Neumann did not respond to the attention of Marino. She was a beautiful and bright young woman, the ideal conquest for a lascivious older man abusing his position of power.

"Did you recall any specific classmates who did have sex with Neumann?"

Winter considered Helene's question before responding. "Oddly, now that I think about it, no. Which is strange because he was notorious as this handsome British professor who was a bit too keen on his female students. And he almost seemed to encourage this image. Praising one student's work to excess, resting a hand on a knee while critiquing a painting. But, curiously, now that I think of it, no one ever actually admitted to sleeping with him. They may just have been too embarrassed. I mean, he even threw parties for students where people got very drunk. So there would have been ample opportunity."

Before speaking again, Helene reached into her backpack and retrieved the intimate photograph from an

168

envelope. She passed it to Winter and asked, "Then what do you make of that?"

Winter examined the photograph in silence, as if staring at the image would force it to reveal its secrets.

"Where did you get this?" Winter asked and then quickly passed the photograph back to Helene, like the glossy paper was toxic.

"I found it among the belongings of Lucy Marino. Possessions that had been discarded by her sister." Helene thought there was no point in explaining her adventures in dumpster diving. It would just confuse the issue.

"Well, it doesn't look like Lucy. You can see a wisp of blonde hair, and she was a brunette."

Helene took another look at the photograph. She hadn't noticed the colour of the woman's hair before, but those were the kind of details someone like Winter, who spent her life with images, would pick out.

"But can you think of any reason why she would have the photo? A picture of Neumann and another woman, perhaps a student?"

"Let me have another look at it." Winter took the photo again but held it by the very edges.

"I can't tell you who the woman was, or why Lucy would have it in her possession. But I do know that the photograph was taken in Neumann's bedroom." The artist held up the photo and pointed to one corner. "You see there, on the wall. Even though it's blurry. That's an original Amelia Grayson. Neumann was very proud of it and would show it off to new students at his parties."

Helene almost took a step back in surprise. It was like the 19th century painter, whom she had gotten to know through her letters, was having a laugh from beyond the grave — or perhaps trying to show the journalist a path forward. She took the photo back from Winter and held it up close. The painting in the picture appeared to be just a blur of land and sky; there was no way to identify it as a Grayson if you hadn't seen it in person.

But she still didn't know how much further this information had gotten her. She couldn't identify the second person in the photo, and she didn't have a good reason why Marino would have the image.

"You don't recognize the tattoo on the arm?" Helene asked hopefully while knowing Winter would not have overlooked such a detail.

"I'm afraid not. I went to art school to learn to paint, not to take my clothes off. I had usually gone home by the time the parties got that interesting."

"I appreciate you sharing what you do know. I only have one last question."

"Sure, although I really should focus on flogging my paintings, even if I don't want to."

"I am wondering if you think Lucy was capable of something like blackmail. Using this photo to get what she wanted."

The artist grimaced slightly before replying. "I think I mentioned before that when I first arrived at the art college, I thought Lucy was marvelous. So passionate. So confident. Everyone wanted to be around her, and I had hoped she would include me in her inner circle. But in the end, I realized we were all part of her performance — or, rather, we were her audience. And she would focus her energy on you if she thought you could help get her what she wanted." The artist paused, perhaps recalling her time at art college.

"It was incredible when you were one of her chosen ones, like the sun was shining directly on you. But after she no longer needed you, you were frozen out."

A well-dressed man in a patterned wool cap came up to the table and started surveying the paintings. Before engaging the potential customer, Winter imparted one last thought to Helene.

"You know that Lucy was a great artist, but she struggled to find her own style. I think when things got desperate at art school, she hoped to steal ideas from the rest of us. And if she was willing to commit artistic plagiarism to get what she wanted, I wouldn't rule out blackmail either."

Helene thanked Winter for her time, tucked the photo back into the envelope, and took one last wistful glance at the breakwater painting.

She wondered what it would be like for Lucy Marino to have the skill to imitate any style of art but no vision of her own. That gap between ability and imagination might make someone furious enough to strike out at those around her. Helene wasn't sure if she was regretful or grateful that she never had the chance to meet Lucy Marino when she was alive. And she also wasn't certain if she was any closer to finding out who had robbed the curator of her bitter existence.

Chapter 22

It was the day before the Grayson exhibition, and Helene was finding it incredibly challenging to concentrate at work. She was supposed to be writing a story about a local sushi restaurant that had started using robots instead of waiters. But the whole concept of automation replacing humans was so disconcerting, she was struggling to remain impartial as journalists were supposed to do. Recently, artificial intelligence had been heralded for its ability to write long, complicated stories combining all manner of facts in a matter of seconds, and she sensed her own career might be in jeopardy. It was true that AI wasn't always known for its accuracy, but this no longer seemed to be a priority in journalism. A digital brain that could churn out salacious headlines and spell most of the names right might be a money maker — that is, if there was any money to be made in the media business anymore.

Helene was still unsure as to whether she should call up Detective Kalinowski and share the compromising photo of Professor Neumann. Even with the help of Rosa Winter, she hadn't managed to figure out the identity of the female figure, and this was a sticking point when it came to her confidence as an investigator.

There had been no more calls from Paola Marino, so she hoped the police had asked a few questions about her sister's death and then let her go. This gave the journalist a little bit of breathing room to keep searching for answers.

Helene was relistening to the interview she had done with the owner of the sushi restaurant, trying to pull the best quotes for her story, when an email notification popped up on her screen. Normally, if she was concentrating on her work, she would ignore a message, unless of course she was waiting for something urgent like a government statement on the removal of a homeless encampment. However, when Helene saw the subject line in this email, she immediately put aside writing the robot story — the world could wait to learn about salmon sashimi being served by a creature with a tin soul.

Re: Family statement on the discovery of two Amelia Grayson paintings

Greetings,

What an absolute delight to receive an inquiry from one of Amelia's fans from across the pond! It is heartening to know her legacy thrives in the quarter of Canada where my great aunt, many times over, made her home more than a century ago. Of course, we have been following the news of the two recently discovered paintings keenly. I would have made the journey to Victoria myself, but a gammy leg from an old riding injury makes sitting for hours on a plane an untenable prospect.

I was delighted to learn you will be attending the public unveiling of the paintings in person, and I would be in your debt if you shared your account of the evening. I know you are also covering it formally as a journalist, but I suspect your private musings would be much more entertaining. I only wonder what Amelia would think of it all! My understanding is that she never had much patience for pomp and ceremony. Raise a teacup of gin in her honour if you can manage it.

I am unavailable for a phone interview before the weekend, as I have committed to a boating excursion, so I have attached a statement to this email which can be quoted for your story. Please attribute it to myself, the great-grandniece of Amelia Grayson, two times over.

Regarding your question about the fate of Amelia's letters, it is my understanding that all of her correspondence had been sent to Victoria about five years ago. I believe the curator at the time made the request to ensure all the key artifacts from her life would be in one place for safekeeping. There was also a suggestion that the letters be turned into a sort of pamphlet, which I surmise you have been reading. I learned about this request for the letters from my mother, who was managing our own records of Amelia until two years ago. That's when she decided to dedicate the remaining years of her life to bowls (or lawn bowling, as you call it), at which point I took over.

However, I must admit to being perplexed by your suggestion that some of the letters were lost in a fire. It is true that I am not yet familiar with every detail pertaining to the life of Amelia, but I feel that a destructive blaze, in which some drawings were even lost, would have stood out in the family lore which has been passed down through the generations.

The good news is I believe copies of all the letters in our possession were made before

174

they were sent overseas, and the files are safely stored in my mother's cellar. I have plans to visit her this weekend, if I can find the patience to be regaled by her tales of victories on the green. I take my cue from Amelia in these circumstances and keep the gin within easy reach.

I was also disturbed to recently learn that a curator has been murdered. It is all quite shocking, and I am not sure what Mother will think when I tell her. I wonder if it is the same curator Mother was dealing with. Do they believe Amelia's paintings were at the heart of the crime, or was it something else entirely? Honestly, I thought Americans were the ones running around shooting each other, not Canadians.

However, if my efforts can help you get to the bottom of the mystery, I am more than eager to be of assistance. I will scan and email copies of all the letters once I locate them at my mother's house.

I hope the opening of the exhibit is a smashing success! I look forward to your musings of the evening.

Sincerely,

Sybil Bancroft

Reading over the email once more, Helene sensed it wasn't just Grayson's letters that had been passed down through the generations but also her feisty spirit. There was even a similar dramatic and slightly antiquated style to the way Sybil used language, like she was an eccentric aristocrat whose "family lore" was filled with fabulous scandals. Helene had to smile at the thought of the painter's dignified relation digging through a dusty cellar for copies of the letters, perhaps surrounded by fading family photos from the Second World War and Christmas panto costumes.

Although she was disappointed not to be able to do a phone interview with the relative for her radio story, at least she had the family statement for her online article. It contained predictable gratitude for the celebration of their ancestor's artistic legacy.

She assumed Lucy Marino was the same curator Sybil's mother had been in contact with. But she was confused about why the family didn't know about the fire the archivist had mentioned. She would follow up with Hana soon, but since it was the day before the two Grayson paintings were revealed to the world, the museum staff member would be too busy to take her call.

Slipping on her desk headphones, Helene forced herself to return to writing the story about the robot waiters. She could have been accused of performing the task like an automaton, her fingers thumping away on the keyboard while her mind rehashed the contents of the email from Grayson's English relative. It was like she had a short circuit in her motherboard causing a continuous loop in her thoughts.

And although Helene was not enthralled by the robot restaurant story, she was at least able to get some entertainment value out of it. Listening to the radio over dinner a few hours later, her children were intrigued by the idea of a droid serving them dinner. Perhaps it reminded them of scenes from *Star Wars*, where glorified talking vending machines kept a wide spectrum of galactic species in drinks. She made a promise to take Oscar and Cleo to the sushi restaurant despite the fact that they would only eat vegetable tempura — raw fish being about as appetizing to the pair as weekend homework.

After the dishwasher was loaded and the leftover food was put away, the journalist found herself unable to relax or sit still. She could not stop thinking about the opening of the Grayson exhibit the following evening. The sense of foreboding and anticipation had intensified over the week.

Since the skies were mostly clear, and there was a potential for a stunning sunset, the journalist grabbed her camera from the table and slung the strap over her neck. If anything could settle her mind, it would be a breakwater outing.

Much to Helene's surprise, as she was getting on her boots by the front door, Oscar shyly asked if he could come along. She told him to grab his sweater and running shoes quickly as the sun was just about to dip below the horizon, a time when the canopied pinks and purples were most vibrant.

Since they were now both old enough to stay home while she went to the breakwater, it was very rare for either of her children to join Helene on a walk, so she didn't dare question Oscar's impulse to keep her company. She loved her son's rambling conversations, flitting from questions about how to survive a zombie apocalypse to a description of the rare and unaccountably adorable axolotl salamander. Her daughter was a gifted artist who drew fantastical pictures of mythical creatures, but she sensed Oscar would be a storyteller one day like her.

The mother and son walked at a swift pace, hoping to get to the end of the breakwater before the climax of dusk. They slipped past couples who were enjoying the evening at a leisurely stroll, people who obviously believed sunsets were to be enjoyed, not pursued like a sighting of the last axolotl. Holding her camera with a firm grip so it wouldn't bounce against her chest, Helene noted that Oscar's short legs were as rapid-fire as his many observations about the universe.

It took about ten minutes for the pair to reach the lighthouse at the end of the concrete edifice. The sun had slipped behind the land but was now lighting up clouds with crimson and rose. The extraordinary sunset had attracted a crowd, and this made it more challenging to get a good shot of the celestial masterpiece.

The platform around the lighthouse was bustling with people, so Helene told Oscar they were going to descend to the lower level of the structure. The eyes of the ten-year-old lit up with excitement as the uneven granite blocks lacked a guard rail and were closer to the lapping waves — much more like the setting of an actual adventure.

Holding Oscar's hand tightly, Helene led them down the metal staircase and onto the slightly slippery blocks. She had a momentary recollection of descending the same steps on the evening she found the body of Lucy Marino, but by focusing on her son and the sunset, she did her best to dismiss those unwelcome thoughts.

Making their way around a corner onto the ledge below the lighthouse platform, the journalist was happily surprised to discover Lee perched on the edge of the blocks. The way he was intensely surveying the horizon reminded her of how the Alberta farmers of her childhood inspected their fields of grain.

Pulling his eyes away from the waterscape to smile at Helene, he then spoke directly to Oscar.

"The sun and sky are putting on a show tonight. Making sure the spring flowers don't get too full of themselves. Giving them a bit of competition. There is more purple in the sky tonight than a meadow of camas."

Because of his experience with anaphylaxis, Oscar usually kept close to his mother's side when they were out of the house, and he was quite wary of strangers. But for some reason, Helene was not surprised when her son made his way over the blocks to stand next to Lee. The older man bent down to Oscar's height, pointing out the highlights of

178

the sunset. The two of them chatted quietly while Helene took the opportunity to capture the brilliant display with her camera. The journalist could not recall the last time she had felt such a sense of tranquility. The tension that had haunted her for most of the day evaporated in the splendour of the evening.

"I was wondering if you wanted to go to a painting exhibition."

The sunset clouds had faded from pink to grey, and the trio was walking back to the metal stairs. Helene had blurted out the question to Lee self-consciously.

Thankfully, he looked neither startled nor uncomfortable. However, Helene could also tell he was going to turn her down.

"I am very honoured that you would ask me to join you. But I don't do well in places with walls. The way some people feel about the water is the way I am about the indoors. Too little space for breathing."

Helene was shocked by this comment. Had Lee sensed her fear of boats? She didn't recall saying anything about it to him.

Revealing a gentle smile and motioning to the world around him, Lee continued. "All the art I need is here in the sky and water. Colours that can never be found at the end of a brush. But you are welcome to join me any evening. Both you and Oscar. It is good to have company after so many years on the ocean."

And so, in the end, his rejection didn't really feel like one. The invitation to spend time on the breakwater together was clearly genuine and heartfelt. She was only a little disappointed she would have to face tomorrow evening alone. She would simply need to get an extra boost of confidence from lipstick and an uncomfortable but stylish pair of shoes.

As if reading her mind, Lee added before turning away, "You are stronger than you know. Both of you. And the things you have faced together, what power it has given, especially a child so young."

Helene and Oscar watched the Coast Guard officer continue to make his way along the lower level of the breakwater before ascending the steps back to the upper pathway themselves. For once her son was quiet on the walk home. Perhaps he was tired out from the evening's exercise. But Helene suspected he was also curious how Lee had known about the fear and trauma of his anaphylaxis. Helene could only wonder at how the man's few words could offer such great comfort.

Chapter 23

Despite the tiring evening walk on the breakwater, the night before the exhibition Helene had a restless, unsatisfying sleep. She spent hours battling blankets as though they were waves trying to drown her. It was as if an angry ocean had followed her home to bed.

In the early morning hours, the faces of all the people possibly connected to the murder of Lucy Marino swirled around in her mind. She kept going over the motives and methods for not only the death of the curator but the poisoning of her friend Alex, but nothing quite made sense.

Professor Neumann caught in a compromising photo.
Paola Marino robbed of an inheritance.
Classmates threatened by old secrets.

At one point, anxious dreams turned to a threatening nightmare. Helene was trying to stay afloat on lurching waves that teemed with flowers instead of fish. As she grasped through the water for some kind of purchase, she began to choke on the petals of orchids, foxglove and even dandelions, all swarming around her like swimming wasps. The journalist woke with a start, gratefully inhaling the bedroom's dark air. And she was also now awake to the fact that, in some way, flowers were a key to unlocking the mystery of the murder.

Helene went through her workday in a kind of trance. Afterwards, had someone asked, she wouldn't have been able to recall what she had eaten for lunch or even what stories she had been working on. And if she had spent the previous night replaying all the conversations she had had with people connected to the murder, then she passed her day by endlessly forecasting how the evening exhibition

181

would unfold. It was a relief to be finally standing in front of her wardrobe selecting an outfit, despite the lingering sense of foreboding.

The public unveiling of the two paintings was being held in a ballroom of the historic Empress Hotel overlooking Victoria's harbour. The Grayson Museum was too cramped to fit all the VIPs, the kind of people who expected waiters carrying silver trays to deliver an endless supply of tiny canapés and generous cocktails.

The Canadian Pacific Railway hotel had been built more than a decade after Grayson disappeared. In fact, the area bordering James Bay would have still been mudflats when she was alive. The construction of the hotel had required parts of the inner harbour to be filled in, and a causeway was built between downtown and James Bay. How the artist might have reacted to the physical transformation of her much-loved landscape would never be known. However, Helene thought the Victorian furnishings and refined atmosphere of the imposing hotel fit with the painter's era.

Wearing a snug, short-sleeved crimson sweater and black pencil skirt that made her feel elegant and professional, Helene pushed through a throng of men in suits to enter the gilded ballroom. Lost in the sea of people for a moment, she experienced a wash of delight and relief at the sight of Alex standing in the centre of the room. A drink in hand, her sleek hair in a beautifully coiled bun, the writer looked like she had as much need for human company as a renaissance statue. Unless, of course, you were her very favourite person to get drunk with.

Alex had been making a steady recovery since the poisoning and had even worked a couple of days at her newspaper that week. Nevertheless, Helene was unsure whether she would be up for an evening out. Judging by the scornful gaze she cast over the crowd, Alex appeared to be much herself again.

"Look who's here," commented Alex after the two friends had exchanged a warm greeting. "He reminds me of a seagull scavenging for garbage on the beach."

Helene glanced in the direction her friend had motioned with her martini glass. She spotted Gary Graham glad-handing a woman in a pantsuit while peering over her shoulder to make sure he didn't miss out on a celebrity sighting. Helene was disappointed to see the disreputable reporter in attendance, and she sensed Grayson would not approve. In her letters, she had expressed disdain for the vacuous praise of a supercilious scribe.

It turned out that Gary Graham was not the only person whose presence was irksome to Helene. In the corner of the ballroom, Professor Neumann was holding court among what appeared to be a flock of students. In a bow tie and shiny waistcoat, his arrogance was palpable from a distance, like the pungent smell of a beach in summer at low tide.

Lifting the drink she had retrieved from a passing waiter, Helene took several long swigs. The evening had already proved interesting, and it had hardly even begun. Feeling the liquor take immediate effect, she almost spilled out what was left in her glass when she spotted Detective Kalinowski striding across the wooden floor, making a beeline for the two journalists. Taking note of Kalinowski's charcoal suit, tailored to show off her stream-lined body, Helene couldn't help but wonder if there was room for a gun under the snug fabric.

"Good to see you up and about," Detective Kalinowski said, addressing Alex first. "I hope you've made a full recovery."

"Physically I'm pretty much good as new," responded the writer. "But I won't be able to relax completely until whoever poisoned me is caught. I even brought my own flask tonight, to fill up my glass, so I can be sure nothing is slipped into my drink."

"I'm going to pretend you didn't tell me that as it strictly isn't legal, but I suppose I can't blame you. But you'll be happy to know I do believe we are getting closer to apprehending the culprit."

"I heard you brought Marino's sister Paola in for questioning," Helene interjected.

"I don't want to know how you know that. But, yes, we wanted to ask about the inheritance. She admits to being angry that her mother left the house to her sister. And she doesn't have an alibi for the window of time the pathologist has given for the murder — the day before the evening you found the body."

"The house in question seems to have changed hands quite a few times in recent years. It originally belonged to the new husband of Lucy's mother," commented Helene.

"Yes, and then he conveniently died a few years later, leaving her mother everything. It seems it was natural causes. A massive stroke. I checked the post-mortem."

"Did he have his own disgruntled children who might have felt cheated by the will?" asked Helene. "Especially after Lucy's mother died and she inherited the house?"

"Seems not," replied Kalinowski. "Just a rich bachelor plum for the picking. At least he didn't die lonely."

Helene wasn't sure the company of two spiteful sisters and a fortune-seeking wife were better than loneliness. But since she had on more than one occasion wished there was someone else to help unload the dishwasher, who was she to judge?

"Good evening, everyone, and thank you for coming."

The journalists' conversation with the detective was interrupted by the woman who had ascended a round temporary stage at the front of the ballroom. Just like the celebration of life for Lucy Marino, this event was once again being emceed by Ivy, the executive director of the museum. The stout woman had traded in her beige smock for a floor-length scarlet dress that was probably bought just for the

184

occasion. Thankfully, the sound system at the Empress Hotel was a bit of an upgrade too, with not a single squeal emitted by the speakers.

The executive director went on to thank the sponsors of the evening and the hotel itself for supporting the exhibition. There was no mention of Lucy Marino, perhaps in an attempt to finally put some distance between the paintings and the murdered curator who had found them.

As Helene observed the well-heeled crowd in attendance, she realized it was the first time she had been in a room with so many people since the start of COVID. Despite the risks, she had decided to forgo wearing a face covering to the event, indulging in one evening of pretending the virus was gone. She just hoped neither she nor her children would have to pay too high a price for her choice.

The mayor of Victoria was now speaking into the microphone, using the opening of the exhibition to bolster her own reputation as a supporter of the arts. In the midst of the politician's description of a new youth arts project coming to a local elementary school attended by vulnerable children, a man carrying a large bouquet of orchids brushed past Helene. Recalling her paralyzing dream of swirling, suffocating petals, Helene inhaled sharply and took several steps backwards. Both Alex and Kalinowski gave her concerned glances, but Helene, recovering quickly, just raised her cocktail glass in explanation, pretending she had spilled the drink on her skirt.

Thankfully, the detective and her friend were distracted by the executive director returning to the microphone, signalling the imminent unveiling of the paintings.

As the crowd watched, two assistants in white gloves ascended the stage, one from each side. Then, in a well-rehearsed, simultaneous flourish, they swept the velvet cloths from the two paintings. A moment later, a collective gasp traversed the room as quickly as a storm's wave. The word FAKE had been scrawled on the front of each canvas in angry dripping letters. The look on the face of the executive director rapidly shifted from a state of pride to one of outrage, and she immediately signalled for the paintings to be covered up once more. But not before several journalists, including Gary Graham, had snapped pictures of the vandalized artworks.

"Can you hold this for me?" The detective handed her glass of water to Alex, who simply nodded in response. Kalinowski headed straight for the stage and the distressed executive director.

The volume of the voices in the room rose dramatically as the guests' shock fuelled declarations of indignation. But Helene could tell by the growing furore in the room that a sedate evening of art and fundraising turning into a national scandal was considered an improvement by many.

Not as quick off the mark as Detective Kalinowski, Helene and Alex both realized they also had a job to do. Placing the drinks they were holding on a side table, the two journalists headed in the direction of the stage. Helene was grateful that when she had shifted her personal belongings from her backpack to a large leather purse for the event, she had decided to bring along her mini digital voice recorder. She winced at the thought of having to rewrite her national story on the unveiling of the paintings in the wake of the vandalism, even though the sensational incident was going to make for irresistible clickbait.

The executive director had been taken into a private office by Detective Kalinowski while the covered paintings had remained in place. Helene assumed they would need to be dusted for fingerprints and other forensic evidence before being moved. The invited guests were slowly being ushered out of the room by other officers who had arrived quickly and were taking down names and numbers. A few journalists stood in the corner of the ballroom, calling in stories to the late desk in their newsrooms.

After about twenty minutes had passed, the executive director finally came out of the office where she had been speaking to detectives and indicated she would make a statement to the press. Taking a swift drink from an abandoned glass of champagne, she then waited for the journalists to turn on their recording devices and form a circle around her.

"Tonight, we have witnessed a crime — an act of violence not only against the legacy of Amelia Grayson, but also against the people of Canada who have come to cherish this exceptional artist's contributions as part of the national fabric of this great country."

Helene was impressed by the eloquence of the woman who was under such incredible pressure. If she had been holding a cigar, she could have been mistaken for Churchill in a red dress. But as the journalist knew, some people thrived in times of crises.

"I am grateful for the wisdom of our museum archivist, who advised me to cover the paintings with a protective glass before the unveiling. So, I can assure you, the artworks are wholly unharmed by the actions of this deranged reprobate."

A murmur spread through the cluster of journalists like a gentle wind. The story of the two paintings could hardly become more thrilling. Seemingly irreparably damaged but then miraculously unscathed.

"Are you going to offer a reward for any clues to the identity of the perpetrator?" Gary Graham shouted out his question while the other reporters were still digesting the information.

"I have total confidence in the police and their ability to find those responsible," the executive director answered. She could not have sounded more curt.

"Even though they haven't figured out who killed your curator?" Graham followed up immediately.

The mention of the murder seemed to spur on the other journalists who had been politely recording the statement. They all began shouting their own questions at the executive director.

"That is all the time I have for questions. I only hope you can remain focused on the proud legacy of Amelia Grayson rather than the action of one unhinged individual."

As she placed her recorder back in her purse, Helene was already mentally reworking her story on the exhibition. Knowing she would have to stay up all night to deliver it to the national editor by the time it was morning in Toronto, she was very grateful that her home office was still set up from the height of COVID. The prospect of spending an evening in an abandoned newsroom held no appeal to the journalist, and this way she could at least be home with her children while they slept. She said a quick, distracted goodbye to Alex, who also faced a night in front of a keyboard.

The hotel staff were working hard to clean up the ballroom as Helene made her way to a side door. The fate of the painting made no difference to their low wages and long hours, she mused, pausing at the door to let a man pushing bouquets of flowers on a trolley pass by. However, as the man leaned forward, the short sleeves of his dress shirt rode up his arms, revealing a large purple tattoo. Helene's eyes widened with alarm, as she immediately recognized the image. On his biceps was a branch of lilac, the same one as was captured in the compromising photo that had been in Lucy Marino's possession before she died. Taking in the man's face as he continued to push the trolley of flowers through the door, she realized it was Benjamin Cornish, the florist who had lied about knowing the curator. In that moment, she cursed her prejudiced brain that had assumed the individual in the photo with Professor Neumann was a woman.

No wonder the successful businessman wanted to disavow any association with the art college. He was possibly the victim of sexual harassment by his professor as well as blackmail by a former classmate.

That only left the question of what Cornish was doing at the unveiling of the paintings. And Helene guessed it was not just to adorn the hall with flowers.

Spinning around to search for Detective Kalinowski, deciding it was finally time to share the compromising photographs, Helene instead ended up face to face with Paola Marino. The baker was swaying from side to side, like a sailor on the high seas. The sister of the dead curator was visibly drunk.

"Not one mention," she slurred. "Not one mention!" the woman said again but in a much louder voice. "It was my sister's night, and they didn't even say her name."

Helene saw that Paola's ranting was attracting the attention of a few reporters who hadn't left yet. Slinging her purse onto her shoulder, the journalist grabbed the arm of the baker and steered her toward an exit.

"Let's get you a taxi," said Helene while looking around for a hotel porter who might offer assistance. Thankfully, a young man in a maroon uniform quickly flagged down a vehicle.

"I know she was a terrible, awful sister, but she was *my* terrible, awful sister," the baker continued to rail, even as Helene opened a cab door and manoeuvred her gently inside, like a delicate soufflé that might collapse at any moment.

"My mother is dead, and now my sister is dead," she continued. From the seat of the taxi, the baker managed to focus on Helene for a moment. "Do you know why my family keeps dying? And why someone would want to destroy the paintings? The paintings my clever dead sister found?"

All good questions, Helene thought as she shut the passenger door. Good questions to which she soon expected to have answers.

The journalist hoped Paola got home safely in the taxi, knowing the woman had a much harder journey ahead — reconciling the grief and guilt of losing a sister who had been so difficult to love. That is, assuming the emotional fireworks the baker had released that evening weren't a double blind to hide a murderous heart.

Chapter 24

"Explain to me again how these photos came into your possession, and this time in a way that makes it sound less like you committed a crime." Detective Kalinowski leaned back in her chair, settling in for a lengthy interview. She had changed out of her designer suit and was once again wearing her green utility vest.

Sitting across the table in a police interview room, Helene was doing her best to frame her dumpster-diving antics in a positive light, but like a floundering politician being grilled on the radio, she knew that some facts couldn't be dressed up.

"I was worried important evidence might be thrown out by Paola Marino. I really did think she might have killed her sister. To be fair, so did you."

"And yet you didn't want to call me. Why?" asked Kalinowski while raising one eyebrow.

"At this point, does it really matter how I got the photos? The fact is they show Professor Neumann and one of his former students in an intimate situation. At first, I assumed it was a woman — that was just my heterosexual bias — but then I saw Benjamin Cornish at the museum event, and he has the same tattoo as the person in the picture. A branch of lilac. He has blond hair, too. And he lied about being at art school with Lucy. Or at least he said he didn't know her. Which makes sense if she had blackmailed him and Neumann."

"I would be cautious about throwing around accusations of blackmail." The detective leaned forward and took a sip of her coffee, appearing to consider the allegations being made by the journalist. And although

Helene hadn't yet been charged with any offences, she was experiencing a rising panic, knowing she could get jail time for interfering with an investigation. Imagining her world being confined to the four grey walls of a cell, she had a sudden intense longing for the wide views of her breakwater excursions. She hoped the police interview wouldn't last too much longer.

"I only wish you had come to me earlier," said Kalinowski after setting down her cup. "The connection to Cornish makes sense of something that has stymied us so far. The hate mail we found in the desk of Professor Neumann and in the office of Lucy Marino had no DNA. But what the papers did all have were traces of orchid. I guess Cornish owns a chain of flower shops." Evidently, the detective had made the decision to continue sharing some details of the investigation. The journalist considered this a good sign.

"He had lots of orchids in the shop I visited. I even ordered some."

"You ordered orchids?"

Helene realized she wasn't helping herself. "This was after you took the hate mail from the museum. So, it couldn't have been me."

"But why did you order orchids?"

Helene ignored the question to which there was no good answer. "Have you interviewed Cornish yet?"

"A couple of officers are bringing him in right now. But he has a lot of store locations, and it is going to take a while to search them all. Did you happen to see any dandelions when you were ordering your orchids?"

"Dandelions? No. They seem a bit low brow for the likes of Cornish. Although I know wildflower bouquets are popular right now. You're looking for a connection to the traces found in Marino's bullet wound?"

"If he was being blackmailed by Lucy Marino, that makes an excellent motive for murder — and, if you were getting too close to uncovering the truth, maybe for sending poisoned chocolates. We are going to have to check his shops for foxglove." The detective added, "I guess I should pick up a book of basic flower identification."

Helene was going to offer to loan Kalinowski the plant guide her children took on their holidays but decided against it.

"What about the paintings? Do you think he vandalized them last night?"

Instead of responding, the police officer picked up her cell phone, which had vibrated twice. Kalinowski read the text message, then stood up abruptly, indicating the interview was over.

"I may want to speak to you again after I question Cornish. We are bringing in the professor too. Just keep your phone on."

Helene stopped herself from explaining that as a journalist and a mother of children with life-threatening allergies, she was always available. Silencing her phone was not an option, even if sometimes she wished it were.

Wanting to make a quick exit from the police station, but also needing to pee, Helene spotted a restroom by the front entrance. After using the toilet, Helene inspected her face and hair in the bathroom mirror. The journalist was curious if any of her colleagues would be able to tell from her frazzled appearance that she had spent her morning in a police interview room. However, the other reporters knew she had been up all night rewriting her story about the paintings, so they wouldn't think twice about the dark circles under her eyes or the stray hairs sticking out from her untidy bun.

Making her way from the bathroom entrance to the police station exit, Helene was temporarily blinded by the sun streaming through the front door glass.

"You bitch!"

The vicious words made the journalist freeze in her tracks. She peered ahead and saw the silhouette of a man, his hands behind his back, probably in handcuffs.

"This is your fault, isn't it? I knew it the moment you came into my shop. Another nosy woman who likes to meddle in other people's business. Just like Lucy!" Benjamin Cornish spat out the name of the curator like it tasted bitter in his mouth.

"I told you to bring him in the back way!" Detective Kalinowski shouted at the officers escorting the florist.

All at once, the days and weeks of frustration, hours spent searching for answers and never finding them, as well as the anger over the threats to her friend and family crested in Helene's heart like a massive rogue wave just before it breaks on the beach.

"So, you killed her?" accused Helene, wanting to put an end to it once and for all. But if she expected Cornish to put up a fight, she was disappointed. Her words could have been a bullet for the way the florist reacted. He was instantly deflated, half collapsing, the two officers on either side holding him up.

"Murder?" Cornish spoke the word with bewilderment, like it belonged to a language he couldn't comprehend. "I didn't murder anyone. I just sent some letters. To scare them. To let them know what it might be like to lose the things they loved. Their careers. Their reputations. Like I lost my art. And they needed to be punished. Professor Neumann, for taking advantage of me when I was so young and naive. And Lucy, for using those photos to force him to turf me out of school. Because I had talent. And she didn't. Not that it did her any good. Not when everyone realized she had no ideas of her own."

"Get him out of here!" commanded Kalinowski, "before he makes a confession we can't use in court."

A diminished Cornish was pushed through a set of doors by the officers.

"And you," Kalinowski directed her next comments to Helene, "Get out of here before I come up with a reason to lay charges. At this point it wouldn't be very hard."

Helene didn't need to be told twice to flee the building, holding onto her backpack tightly as she raced down the front steps. Her only thought as she hurried toward her car was that, clearly, spending a lifetime arranging flowers was no cure for bitterness — if anything, it made a rich soil for fury to flourish.

Although she was weary from rewriting her national article to include the vandalism of the two Grayson paintings, Helene thought she should stop in at the office before heading home to sleep. A colleague had put together a radio piece for the early morning news run, but she wanted to make sure they didn't need any more details.

The previous evening, after taking a taxi home herself, Helene had tried again to get in touch with Kalinowski. However, the police officer had been too busy interviewing witnesses at the hotel to take her call. So, the journalist waited until she had rewritten her story and sent it off to the national editor before texting the detective in the early hours of the morning. By the time she had gotten out of the shower, trying to wash away her exhaustion, she had received an unwelcome, if unsurprising, invitation to visit the police station right away.

When Helene entered the newsroom, she said hello to several of her colleagues, who looked up from their computer screens. She could only imagine they had all been rehashing the events of the previous night over their coffee — and, like all keen journalists, they were likely envious they had not been present at the unveiling themselves. Careers had been made by being at the right place when things went very wrong.

"Helene, in my office," Riya called through the open door, not bothering to get out of her chair.

Dropping her backpack onto her desk, Helene grabbed a glass of water before making her way into her producer's office. She did not wait for an invitation to sit down. She figured she had earned it.

"Well done on rewriting the article last night. We got ours up before any other station. And I've heard from the web people it's getting a lot of traffic. It's number two on the national site right now, just behind a story about Russia's threats to invade Norway. You are up there with Putin." Most people would prefer not to have their accomplishments ranked against the fame of a leader accused of war crimes, but Helene took her producer's remarks as they were intended, a convoluted compliment only a journalist could appreciate. But as usual, glory in a newsroom lasted about as long as a weather report.

"So, what's next? I know you were still investigating the murder of the curator who found the two paintings. Do you have an update on that?" Riya took off her glasses, rubbed the bridge of her nose, and then put them back on, fixing her gaze on Helene.

"I believe the police will have a breakthrough soon. My sources have let me know they have a very strong suspect. Someone connected to Lucy Marino's days at art school." Helene wanted to give her producer enough information to keep her happy without revealing any names.

"I'm glad to hear you're cultivating contacts in the police station. Those can be valuable."

"It helps that I was the one who discovered the body."

The producer and the journalist just stared at each other as the words hung in the air. Helene assumed it was the total exhaustion of her mind and body which had caused her to blurt out the admission. She sensed her career was going to go from an all-time high to a new low in record time.

"You found the body? Of the curator?" Riya asked, clarifying the facts before moving to judgment.

"I'm sorry I didn't tell you earlier. I was afraid you wouldn't let me cover the story."

What happened next left Helene slightly dumbfounded.

"I love it," said Riya, with feverish delight in her eyes. "I think we can use it. I mean, once the murder has been solved by the police, I can see another national story. First-person view, 'Journalist's Close Encounter with True Crime.' People will eat it up."

Clearly her producer did not have an issue with the ethics of a journalist covering a story to which they had a connection. Helene supposed that these days, principles had to take second place to maintaining the attention of an audience, especially when there was an abundance of free internet animal videos featuring every creature, from orcas to axolotls.

Helene was debating whether this was the right moment to disclose to Riya that someone had also attempted to poison her, but then the phone in her pocket rang. Pulling it out and glancing down at the screen, she saw it was Kalinowski calling.

"It's the police," Helene stated.

"Go, go, go!" Riya said, waving her out of the office. "This is your only story now."

The journalist quickly made her way into the boardroom for some privacy before picking up the call.

"Helene speaking," she answered, silently praying she wasn't being called back to the police station for another interview. She really needed to get some sleep.

"I just wanted to let you know we wrapped up the initial interview with Cornish."

"And did he admit to everything?"

"That's why I'm calling. He came clean about sending the hate mail to Marino and Neumann, I guess he had been doing it for many years. Like he said when confronting you, she had used the photos to get him kicked out of art school.

197

She considered him a threat of some kind. The class competition. And I guess having a successful chain of flower shops never made up for that."

"Does he know how she used the photos against Neumann?"

"Cornish thinks she originally tried to use them as leverage to allow her to stay in art school. But then he says Marino was caught copying the project of another student. At that point there was nothing he could do to protect her besides hush it up."

Helene knew he must have struggled to keep a lid on Lucy's artistic plagiarism as Rosa Winter had vague knowledge of it. And then another idea occurred to her.

"But she held onto the photos. And used them later."

"What are you thinking?"

"Well, her credentials were always a bit weak to get a job as a curator at the Grayson Museum. She didn't have a degree of any kind. Even the archivist at the museum seemed a little confused by her early career success."

"You think she might have forced Neumann to use his influence to get her the job?"

"From everything I have come to learn about Marino, it sounds exactly like something she would have done. I can almost understand why Cornish sent the hate mail."

"But that's why I called. He's admitted to writing and sending the letters and even writing the word *bitch* in the memorial book on the day of the museum ceremony for Marino."

Helene thought back to the service she had attended at the gallery at the start of her own investigation, and she vaguely recalled a man placing flowers around the room. It must have been Benjamin Cornish, using his access as a florist as an opportunity to scrawl the vicious word.

"He's also taken responsibility for vandalizing the paintings. He says he has no idea whether they are genuine or not, but he just wanted to embarrass Neumann who had authenticated them, and damage Marino's legacy as a curator."

"I think he has managed that much."

"But he hasn't admitted to murdering her. He swears he's never touched a gun in his life. Says they terrify him. And my instinct as a police officer is he's telling the truth."

Helene sensed what was coming next.

"You still need to be careful. The killer probably believes they got away with it. Which may make them even more dangerous. You need to go home and stay there until I interview Cornish again. If he does confess to murder, I'll let you know right away."

Since going home meant going to bed, Helene put up no protest. She knew she should be worried about the warning from Kalinowski, but she was more concerned about collapsing from exhaustion than being attacked by a killer.

April 16, 1886

My dearest Constance,

If you only knew the ardent effort it takes to still my hand to put pen to paper. I am quite unsettled from the events of yesterday, and although I do not wish to cause you worry, I must be allowed to share these happenings with another, if only to create a better understanding of them in my own mind. A warning before beginning: this will be a lengthy missive, so you must find a private place of repose before surveying the contents.

Perhaps the most curious part of the shocking day is that although it did end in such a strange and disquieting way, it was not without almost miraculous pleasures.

I do not expect you to condone my decision to arrange another boating excursion with my companion, Charlie. I know you will think it is not fitting behaviour for a woman of my position, much less without a chaperone. But I am starting to wonder, if I am to follow all the rules of society, whether I will ever enjoy any true companionship again. I know my housekeeper and Margaret are of the same mind, that I should spend my days drinking tea and gossiping about who is wearing the latest hats.

We set out from the beaches of James Bay just after first light in Charlie's fishing boat, and I have to admit, the smell of the vessel was something to which I may never become accustomed. However, the splendour of the sunshine reflecting off the rolling waves soon captivated my senses. Picture me sitting at the helm like a restless figurehead, taking in the view all around.

Our journey of almost one hour brought us to a narrow island off the coast, a landscape mostly occupied by seabirds of various plumage. I was thankful to have worn my walking boots that morning, all the better for scrambling over the rocks and moss.

Charlie had the foresight to pack us a repast of bread, dried salmon, and berries. It may have been that the resplendent view was the greatest of seasonings, but I have never tasted morsels so rich in flavour. Then the hours seemed to slip by as easily as clouds, the ocean waves entertaining us better than a theatre pantomime. I am most grateful that Charlie is immune from the compulsion to fill silence with nattering conversation, the few words he speaks carry weight and great meaning.

As you can well imagine, when I returned to my home I was in a state of almost rapture, all my faculties awakened by the ocean sojourn. And it was in this state of ecstasy that I was confronted with a ruin of violence that had been visited on the studio in my absence.

Paint strewn across the floors, sketches ripped into tattered shreds, and most alarming of all, a preliminary canvas stabbed with a jagged knife. Immediately it came to mind that the intruder might still be present in the house, so I rushed to the drawer where I had put away the weapon Father insisted I bring on my journey to this new land, the cold metal untouched since my arrival. I slipped the heavy device into the pocket of my dress as I searched the house for an unwelcome visitor.

Only after I had searched every nook and cranny of each room did I give myself an opportunity to rest and consider the fury wreaked on my art and home. It was in *that moment I did take seriously a proposition which Charlie had made to me while we were reclined on those sun-warmed island rocks.*

He told me of a log cabin he built in the upper regions of Vancouver Island, a place mostly not yet explored by Europeans. He wishes me to pack a valise of paint, brushes, and canvases, and journey there for a summer's rest.

I know you will consider me quite mad for even entertaining the idea of embarking on this adventure with a man whom I have known for only a short while. But I admit to feeling an unrivalled joy and peace when I am in his company. I long for your approval but know I may depart without it. Do not yet despair, my mind is not quite yet made up. But perhaps this excursion is the best way to escape from those who wish me harm. I await your answer with an unsettled heart.

With steadfast affection,

    Amelia

Chapter 25

As Helene read over Amelia Grayson's letter to her sister Constance, she tried to fully comprehend all the implications of the words written down more than a hundred years ago. Fear and delight were close companions on the page.

A scandalous invitation to run away.

A weapon in a drawer.

A soul who wished the artist harm.

Resting in bed after an intense morning nap, trying to recover from the fatigue of a night without sleep, the journalist considered who might have vandalized Grayson's studio. The ex-fiancé, Howard Weatherington, who had attended her art exhibition, still hounding the woman who had jilted him at the altar? Or perhaps her friend Margaret had grown jealous of the time the artist was spending in the company of the fisherman. Helene thought there was probably no way to ever know for sure, so she turned her attention to the email from Sybil Bancroft that had accompanied the final letter.

Greetings,

I hope the gala for the unveiling of the paintings was a brilliant affair. I haven't yet had the opportunity to survey the news coverage, but I look forward to reading your article with great anticipation.

I have attached a copy of the last letter known to be written by Amelia. However, when I mentioned my search for this correspondence to my mother, she had a tale to tell.

It turns out the envelope containing this letter went unopened for more than fifty years. Amelia's sister Constance had become quite ill with tuberculosis in the late spring of 1886. She always did have trouble with her lungs. As you know, this was also shortly before Amelia went missing. It seems the letter was tucked away with the others, probably by a servant who didn't want to disturb her indisposed mistress, and the communication must have been long forgotten by the time news of Amelia's disappearance finally reached England. It was Constance's daughter Minnie who finally discovered the unread letter almost half a century later.

We have always presumed Amelia drowned, as her favourite shawl, knit by her sister, was discovered on a beach near her home. But maybe this is not what occurred at all? This letter certainly raises some other possibilities. Perhaps she ran away with this fellow Charlie, who sounds like a marvellous breath of fresh air at a time of corsets and chaperones. Or maybe she was murdered by the same person who destroyed the paintings in her studio! I do wonder how differently the local authorities would have handled her disappearance if this letter had been shared with them.

No matter, I find it absolutely smashing that Amelia had a bit of a dalliance before she disappeared forever. After rejecting a society marriage, she was so exclusively focused on her art, and she became a celebrated success because of it. But as my mother would say, we all need a bit of bloody fun. Speaking of which, I'm off to watch the races. If I can't ride the nags anymore, at least I can have a flutter. Hope I pick a winner this time.

Please remember to send me the link to your article!

Sincerely,

Sybil Bancroft

Helene smiled once again at the jaunty tone of the descendant of Amelia Grayson's sister. She hoped one day she might meet Sybil Bancroft. The woman sounded like someone who really did know how to take life by the reins.

The journalist reflected for a moment on whether it was time to take her kids on a proper vacation, perhaps even to England. Travelling as a single mother had always seemed too daunting, especially air travel with life-threatening allergies. And then COVID had shut down any thoughts of leaving Vancouver Island for several years. But Cleo was old enough now to help her manage packing, and Oscar knew how to avoid the most dangerous allergens. Remembering the delight on their faces during the whale-watching expedition, the sheer joy of an utterly new experience, Helene decided to explore the idea of an overseas vacation once Marino's murderer was finally arrested. Or when they confessed, if it was Benjamin Cornish.

The one prospect that did give Helene pause was telling Grayson's relation how badly the unveiling had gone. How would she ever explain why the vengeful florist had tried to vandalize the two paintings? It was all so complicated and sordid. A professor seducing his student. A compromising photo used to destroy an art class rival. Helene decided to put off breaking the bad news, choosing to let Sybil think the event had been a success a little longer. And it was already nighttime in the UK, so hopefully Sybil would not search the internet until the morning.

Getting herself out of bed to eat a breakfast that was in fact a lunch, Helene made her way into the kitchen. Her children were both visiting friends for the last day of spring break, and the journalist was grateful to have a quiet house to herself. Eggs seemed like the best option for her confused stomach. But first she made herself a large mug of coffee to clear the fog still lingering in the corners of her mind.

She knew there was no pressure for her to work for the rest of the day, but her own natural curiosity demanded she follow up on last night's events. Helene was grateful when the archivist picked up her call to the main line of the museum after two rings.

"How are you doing, Hana? Have you been able to get some sleep?" Helene could only imagine what the past twelve hours had been like for anyone connected to the museum.

"Not really. It's been chaos. Ivy is taking calls from the national press. And now we are being asked by the police to retest the paintings. It's untenable. Our reputation is being called into question. The only good news is I understand the police have arrested someone. Do you know anything about that?"

"Yes. I'm not sure how much I can say. But it was a man your curator, Lucy Marino, knew a long time ago. Someone she had hurt. And this was his way of getting revenge. Trying to destroy the legacy of what she discovered," explained Helene.

"Of course, Marino was at the heart of this. The museum never should have hired her. Ivy went against my advice at the time. And look now what that woman has done. Causing more trouble, even from the grave."

Helene was a little taken aback by the archivist's criticism. Hana had never shared any doubts about Lucy's skills as a curator before.

Hoping to distract the aggrieved woman, Helene decided to share her good news. "By the way, I managed to track down the last letter Amelia Grayson wrote to her sister in England. Her relation sent me a copy. And boy, does it pack a punch. Raises a whole bunch of questions about her disappearance. I only wonder why Marino didn't share this letter with you — she had requested it from the family a few years ago."

"You've got the last letter?" The archivist was very interested, but in a way that sounded slightly manic rather than pleased. Helene put it down to the turmoil and stress of a sleepless night.

"Well then, we should meet," Hana continued. "After work. You can understand that, as an archivist, I am desperate to read the letter."

"Are you sure today? With everything else going on?"

"It will give me something positive to think about. I absolutely insist. The weather is supposed to be good. Perhaps we could meet along the beach?"

"What about the breakwater?" Helene suggested. The ocean air would help her recover. She might take the opportunity to interview the archivist for a follow-up story about the paintings.

"Perfect. That's so near to where Amelia used to take her walks. Very fitting."

Helene spent the rest of the day ineffectually cleaning the house, picking up one of her son's toys only to leave it in a random spot in a different room. She would occasionally take breaks to read other articles about the vandalism at the unveiling of the paintings. When it was time to collect her kids, her house wasn't any more organized, but at least she was confident no competing media had a new angle on the shocking story of the exhibition.

However, with the arrival of evening, the choice of the breakwater as a place to meet Hana had become less appealing. An afternoon breeze was now a gusting wind, chasing the last of the cherry blossoms from the trees across the street.

Before leaving, Helene told Cleo through a closed bedroom door she would be gone for about an hour. Getting no reply from her daughter, she did receive several clinging hugs from Oscar who didn't want her to go out. She did her best to reassure him, saying she would be back home well before bedtime. But something in his worried look made her consider missing her appointment with the archivist. Thankfully, Cleo chose that moment to come out of her room and ask her brother to play a round of his favourite board game.

The journalist then packed a protective windsock to block the sound of the gusting air from her microphone, although she now doubted whether it would be possible to interview the archivist outside at all. Pulling on thick gloves and her wool hat, Helene mused that Victoria's weather was as capricious as affection from a teenager, never to be taken for granted. A few minutes later, as she was making the blustery trek from her house to the start of the breakwater, Helene wished she had listened to her impulse to stay home.

"Should we walk along the lower level? It might offer us some protection from the wind." The suggestion was made by Hana who had arrived promptly at 7:00 at the start of the breakwater.

"Why don't we just go into the café instead?" Helene countered. "We can talk more easily and do an interview as well. We've both had a long day after an even longer night, and a cup of tea or something stronger sounds good to me."

"Let's do the walk first and the interview after. The air is so invigorating this evening."

Helene was surprised by the archivist's enthusiasm for exercise in the belligerent weather. But maybe a close encounter with the elements was welcome when you spent your days sorting file folders.

It wasn't the first time Helene had walked along the breakwater during a severe wind, but she had never taken the lower level when the waves were this high. A few times the water splashed over the granite blocks in front of her, narrowly missing her sneakers. She called ahead to Hana to suggest ascending to the upper level in order to stay dry. But gusts of air whipped away her words, like seagulls snatching food from an unwary tourist.

The blustery sojourn of the journalist and archivist was accompanied by the hum of the wires which lined the breakwater railings above. This morose thrumming occurred when the wind was most intense, as though the exposed structure was voicing its own complaint. The low howl, like a warning of danger ahead, only added to the hostile atmosphere of the evening and heightened Helene's regret for agreeing to the excursion in the first place.

For about ten minutes Helene had been walking with her head down, scanning the wet rocks in front so as to not slip and stumble, and that meant she didn't notice the archivist had come to a halt until she almost bumped into her. The pair had reached the end of the breakwater, and Helene realized she had already passed the place where she had discovered Lucy Marino's body. She shuddered briefly as the image of the dead curator's halo of sodden hair flashed through her mind.

"Can I see the letter?" The archivist yelled over the wind, holding her gloved hand out in expectation.

Helene was utterly confused by this request. Hana wanted to see Amelia's last letter now? Why not wait until they were inside the café, where the wind and the water couldn't reach them?

However, the archivist did not withdraw her hand, intractable in her desire to see the document at that moment.

Both bewildered and exhausted, Helene didn't have the energy to protest, so she took off her backpack and fished out the papers.

But what the archivist did with the printout of the letters after snatching them from Helene was even more perplexing. Taking only a moment to quickly glance at the pages, Hana then tossed them away into the angry wind.

Helene watched as the papers did a brief dance in the air before plunging into the ocean waves where they immediately slipped below the surface.

Hana leaned forward and shouted into Helene's ear, "And now we wait."

Helene was going to ask what was going on when she felt the archivist thrust a hard object against her ribs. Glancing down, she saw a small antique pistol in the woman's hand. The journalist understood the time for asking questions had passed. Neither the wind nor the archivist were going to let her voice be heard.

Chapter 26

Any progress Helene had made overcoming her fear of boats during the whale-watching expedition with her children was utterly undone by being forced onto a vessel at gunpoint during raging winds in the dying light of day.

Only a few minutes had passed after the archivist had pulled a weapon on the journalist before a boat pulled up next to the end of the breakwater, with Jeff at the helm. Shocked to discover the Coast Guard officer was in league with the archivist, Helene desperately glanced around for any sign of Lee, hoping he might intervene. However, she quickly realized she was on her own.

The vessel had a protective rubber bumper on the left side to keep it from hitting against the breakwater, and Helene had to scramble over the slippery surface and gunwale. She was hit by several waves in the process and was now wet through to her skin and shivering intensely. Once the archivist had made a surprisingly agile leap from the breakwater to the vessel, the Coast Guard officer pushed the throttle all the way forward. Helene felt her chest tighten in fear as the breakwater rapidly retreated in the distance.

With the archivist pointing the gun at Helene, the boat travelled in the direction of the American coast. The journalist's mind raced to make sense of what was going on while her body became even more rigid from cold.

The archivist had used an antique gun to murder Marino.

The Coast Guard officer was somehow connected to the crime.

Amelia's last letter might just cost Helene her final breath.

The journalist wasn't sure exactly how much time had passed before Jeff killed the engine of the boat. They appeared to be at a midpoint between Vancouver Island and the Olympic Mountains. The closest vessel was a freighter about half a kilometre away. The massive ship dwarfed the Coast Guard boat, and Helene knew there was no hope of signalling the crew for help. No dramatic rescue was in the cards from that quarter.

It was a small mercy when the archivist indicated Helene should move into the cabin where there was some shelter from the wind. While the journalist held her hands over a small heater, trying to restore some feeling to them, the archivist told Jeff she needed to speak to him outside.

As he followed the archivist out of the cabin, Helene examined the face of the officer she had considered an honest man. He wouldn't meet her eye, an indication he wasn't entirely free from the guilt of his involvement in her kidnapping.

Once Jeff was outside on the deck, the wind whipping his thick blond hair in every direction, the archivist leaned in as if to say something in his ear. However, Helene watched in horror as Hana instead stuck the gun in his chest and shot him point blank. The Coast Guard officer was close enough to the gunwale that as he collapsed Hana simply pushed him over the edge and into the water. She performed the motion with the same fluid movement as she might return a stray file to a drawer. Helene was both impressed and terrified.

"I'm sorry you had to see that," apologized Hana as she re-entered the cabin, pointing the gun at Helene. "It had to be done. I have decided to tie up all the loose ends tonight."

"And that includes killing me too?" Helene couldn't help but ask.

212

"Unfortunately, I don't really see any way around that. Perhaps if you hadn't insisted on getting Amelia's last letter from the family, you could have been spared. But now you might wreck everything." The archivist sounded surprisingly regretful for someone who had just committed another murder.

"But first I want to explain it all to you. So you can see why I didn't have a choice. You may be the only person who ever knows what I've done. It's important for someone to understand. You will be my archive. At least until you die."

Even though Helene was borderline hypothermic and in conversation with the woman who planned to kill her, she couldn't help but slip into her role as a journalist. The confession of the archivist might be the last story she would ever bear witness to. And the familiar act of asking questions brought some comfort in what could be the last hour of her life.

"Why did you kill Jeff?" The journalist thought asking about the murder she had just witnessed was as good a place as any to start.

"He needed to be punished. For what he did with Lucy. For his role in putting the art and legacy of Grayson into jeopardy."

"And what exactly did he do?"

"He helped Lucy smuggle paintings to the US."

"And you killed her for doing that?"

"Among other things. But I really don't understand why everyone is making such a fuss about her death. She was a cheat and a blackmailer. Her own sister didn't even like her. Or her partner in crime. When I told Jeff I had killed her, he wasn't particularly upset. He just wanted to make sure the murder couldn't be traced back to him."

Helene recalled how the Coast Guard officer was the first to show up after she had discovered Lucy's body. At the time there was no way she could have guessed he was involved in criminal activity with the dead woman. And she

213

remained absolutely certain Lee didn't know what was going on.

"So, they were smuggling paintings? I thought her death might be somehow connected to forgeries. I kept hearing about her talent for imitation."

"It was both. They were smuggling genuine paintings after she had replaced them with forgeries. Marino knew she was never going to be a great artist, but she saw an opportunity to use her skills as a mimic. I think that's why she became a curator, to gain access to originals. She set about creating virtually perfect copies of Grayson's paintings, replaced the originals with her fakes at the museum, and then sold the genuine works to collectors who lacked any scruples. The fact that Grayson left behind instructions on how she made her own paints from flowers also allowed Lucy to create colours that would pass any test for authenticity. Poppies, geraniums, even dandelions."

At the mention of dandelions, Helene made the connection to the traces of the yellow petals found in Marino's fatal wound. The antique gun and bullets must have been stored in a drawer with old paints made from flowers for more than a century.

"And Jeff used his authority as a Coast Guard officer to take the paintings across the water in a boat to Washington?" Helene allowed herself to be impressed by the criminals. She only wished she would live to write a story about them — her producer Riya would love it.

"Yes, the pockets of American collectors of Pacific Northwest art apparently run pretty deep."

"But how did you catch them at it?" asked the journalist.

"You aren't the only one who likes to walk the breakwater in the evening. I have seen you there often enough, although you have never noticed me — one advantage of being an unattractive middle-aged woman: you are basically invisible to the world. Including other women." The archivist spoke these last words with amusement rather than any bitterness.

"Anyways, one time I saw them loading up crates at the docks. And I somehow doubted Lucy had taken up a part-time job as a longshoreman. When I confronted her, she brazenly bragged about what she had done. How she used trips on a whale-watching boat to signal the smugglers. The way she followed Grayson's formulas to make paints. She knew I wouldn't say anything to the police that would put the reputation of the museum in jeopardy. And she said that selling the real paintings and leaving behind the fakes was her way of sticking it to the art world, the world that had rejected her."

Caught up in their intense exchange, both the archivist and the journalist were jarred by the ringing of a cell phone. Helene could only assume the effects of hypothermia had caused her to forget the phone was in her pocket, and she silently cursed herself for not finding an opportunity to call or text for help.

"It will be my children," blurted out the journalist before the archivist had a chance to react. "I'm always home by bedtime, before it gets dark. They'll be worried. Might even call the police." Helene hoped the archivist didn't have a lot of experience with children who were more likely to watch an extra episode of their favourite show than worry about why their parents were late. "I have to answer the phone. Say something. Anything."

Keeping the gun aimed at Helene, the archivist nodded. "Okay, you can talk for a minute. But if you let them know you are with me, or what's going on, I will track them down once I am done with you."

If the archivist had hoped to subdue Helene by threatening her children, she would have been disappointed to know it had the opposite effect. At that point the numbness of Helene's hands was nothing compared to the ruthless chill that swept through her heart. The archivist clearly didn't know anything about parents either. Or what happened when you posed a danger to their young.

"Hello, sweetheart," Helene said, relieved to hear it was Cleo on the other end of the line. She wasn't sure Oscar could handle what she was about to say. "I'm sorry I'm late, I just got caught up taking too many photos. It was such an incredible sunset. I'll be home soon. But can you please make yourself and your brother a bedtime snack — maybe a peanut butter sandwich for you? And your brother might like a banana."

Helene hung up before her daughter could reply. She prayed her message had been understood.

"Give me the phone," demanded the archivist, grabbing the device and throwing it out the cabin window into the water.

Helene knew she now needed to buy herself as much time as possible, and the best way to do that was to keep Hana talking.

"What about the two paintings Lucy discovered? Are they real? Or more fakes she painted?"

The archivist smiled and shrugged. "Honestly, who knows. The paints and canvases all passed the authenticity tests, but that doesn't mean a lot since Grayson also left behind half-finished works. Lucy could have stripped down a canvas and painted a new landscape on them. The works could be genuine, or they could be fakes — all part of Lucy's plan to be famous for finding them. That's my one regret in killing her. I'll never know if they are Grayson's own paintings. And as an archivist dedicated to recording the truth, that's more than a little irritating. But the most important thing is the reputation of the museum, and Grayson's legacy has not been tarnished. Which is why I will need to kill you as well."

"I still don't exactly follow how I am a threat." If the journalist was going to be murdered, she at least wanted to know the reason.

"You wouldn't leave those stupid letters alone. I knew I should have destroyed the pamphlets before anyone spotted them. I didn't even realize they were still in Lucy's office when I let you look around. My mistake. Which you will pay for. You see, Lucy had done the same thing as you. Gotten the letters sent over from England. She had shown them to me, and she was so delighted by the scandalous details. She was going to sell the pamphlets containing the earlier letters, and then, after the unveiling of the two paintings, reveal the final correspondence. How Grayson was planning to run away with a fisherman. Abandoning her studio and her growing reputation as one of Canada's preeminent painters. I begged Lucy not to do it. But she wouldn't listen. So, she really did have to die. If I had let those details get out, Grayson would have just been seen as another flighty woman, giving up her true artistic calling for romance. The story would probably have been made into a movie. I couldn't let that happen. I had to protect her reputation as a feminist. As an example to all women. To not be distracted from her true calling by something as ridiculous as love. You see, I had a higher cause." From the way the archivist was talking about preserving Grayson's legacy as a painter, Helene could tell she was justifying her own devotion to the world of art. To question Grayson's purpose was to create doubt about how the archivist had spent her own life. Never having children. Never finding love. Dedicating her days to the Grayson Museum.

"And then you came along and tracked down the same foul letter. I couldn't trust you to keep quiet — a journalist whose job it is to share salacious news with the world. It's your own fault."

Helene was tempted to point out that this was blaming the victim for their own murder, which hardly seemed fair. But she knew her life depended on making the archivist feel like Helene understood the motives behind her actions. So that the archivist would continue her confessional until help arrived — assuming her daughter had understood her message and gotten help.

"I think once the fuss over your disappearance has all died down, I may need to travel to England myself and finally destroy the original copy of Amelia's last letter. I have always wanted to visit Yorkshire." The archivist smiled, seemingly at the thought of overseas travels.

"And it was you who sent the poisoned chocolates?" Helene was exhausted from shivering, but she forced herself to keep asking questions.

"Yes, apologies to your friend. How was I to know you would give them to her? I was originally quite pleased with my choice of foxglove, an extension of Grayson's own use of flowers for paint. But I now believe poisoning is really a second-rate way of killing someone — so imprecise, and such delayed gratification. Grayson's gun is much more efficient and somehow fitting."

"But Amelia never wrote she was going to give up art if she went away with her friend Charlie. It sounded like she would have taken her paints along to his cabin in the woods."

Helene was desperately switching from one topic to another, and she knew her brain was shutting down from cold. But thankfully the archivist didn't seem to notice.

"Then why did the world never hear from her again? No, I prefer to believe she drowned in the ocean by accident or by design. A fate not dissimilar from your own. Speaking of which, it's time I got back to land. It's going to be too dark to see anything soon. I am quite new at steering boats. Jeff taught me a few things, but I am also going to have to crash the boat onto the shore, as though it's been abandoned. Could be a bit tricky for a beginner. Thankfully I have always been a good swimmer, and I will be long gone before the authorities show up."

Stepping across the cabin to shove the gun directly into Helene's side, the archivist nudged the journalist out of the cabin and onto the deck.

At least a half hour had passed since the sun had dropped below the horizon, and the only light left in the dusky sky were some patches of pink reflecting off the clouds. Facing the gunwale, the tip of the gun now pressing into her spine, Helene looked down into the foreboding ebony depths of the ocean.

Was her fear of boats a foreshadowing of how she would die?

Would a bullet be preferable to drowning?

Did she have the courage to control her own death?

"I'm glad it was you I got to explain everything to." Hana's voice broke into Helene's morbid thoughts. "We are both storytellers. The archivist and the journalist. I do wish I could let you live. But Grayson's legacy must remain intact."

"But what will the world think? Why did I disappear? What about Jeff? What if they find our bodies? Or don't?"

"Before I brought you out here, Jeff was kind enough to write up an email inviting you to join him on the water this evening as part of your coverage of drug smugglers using boats. That's because he believed I planned on killing only you. He wasn't the brightest fellow — the good-looking ones often aren't. And like everyone else, he underestimated me. I asked for a cut of the money he and Marino had made selling the paintings. He thought it would end there. As if I cared about the money."

Sensing time was running out, Helene knew she had a decision to make. Wait for the finality of the bullet to rip through her body, or cling to the smallest hope of survival by embracing her greatest fear — diving into the ocean. Ultimately the choice was clear: she would govern her own fate, even to the end. But she wasn't going into the ocean alone.

Quickly turning around, pushing the gun aside, Helene wrapped her arms around the archivist, pulling the woman who had threatened the lives of her children into the water as she slipped overboard herself.

As her body plunged deep into the water, the shock of the cold almost made it impossible to breathe. Panicking as she struggled to figure out which direction was up, Helene watched the underwater archivist point the now-useless gun in her direction. Hana was determined to get her prey even as she faced her own death. Then the water grew murky, and a roar filled the ears of the journalist. She wondered if this was what it felt like to drown. It was remarkably noisier than she had expected.

When a hand reached down from above to grasp her flailing limbs, she had no way of knowing if perhaps she was already dead and was being claimed by an angel. But when her head broke the surface, the relief on the face of her friend Lee as he pulled her to safety made it evident she was still among the living.

Chapter 27

Helene had spent enough time in hospital rooms with her children to recognize the familiar beeps of heart monitors and the patter of the plastic clogs of nurses, even without opening her eyes. Only when she felt a small, familiar hand squeezing her own did she decide it was time to let in the light. The first thing she saw after fully awakening was Oscar leaning on the right side of her hospital bed. Cleo was to her left, standing back a little, but her face just as anxious.

"You clever girl," Helene stated in a hoarse voice. She reached out her other hand to Cleo, who eagerly grasped it. "You knew just what to do."

"I'm not an idiot," said her daughter with a smirk. "There is no way you would tell me to eat peanut butter. And then you added in bananas for Oscar, just to make sure I understood that something was really wrong."

"Who did you phone?"

"Alex, of course. And she called some kind of detective she knew."

Helene squeezed the hands of both of her children, wishing she had the energy to sit up properly and hug them. But she was so very tired.

"I was really scared, Mom," whispered Oscar.

"I know, sweetheart. And I am sorry for that. But it's all over now. We can go home very soon." Never before had the thought of her messy house and piles of laundry and dishes been so enticing. But she had come very close to not seeing it all again.

The family reunion was abruptly interrupted by the curtain around the bed being swiftly pulled back. A nurse holding a clipboard approached Helene, first checking the flow of the IV into her arm.

"How are you, lass?" The health care worker had a Scottish accent, which Helene, in her stupor, thought was quite delightful.

"Happy to be alive. But also like I could sleep forever."

"That'll be the hypothermia. Your body is sure to be worn out from trying to keep warm. We're giving you a dose of fluids to make you right again."

"When can I go home?"

"You're tired of us already?" joked the nurse. "You haven't even had a taste of the food. Probably best to give it a miss anyway. Sounds like you've had enough near-death experiences in the past twenty-four hours."

"Can I join the party?" Detective Kalinowski had appeared at the corner of her hospital bed. "How is the patient?" she asked the nurse.

"Not bad for a barmy woman who decided to take a plunge in the Pacific Ocean in March. If that's someone's idea of fun, I could recommend a few beaches in Aberdeen for your next holiday. Practically tropical."

Not wanting her kids to get scared by the details being shared by the nurse, Helene asked Cleo to take her brother to the waiting room for a few minutes. The sight of her teenage daughter wrapping her arm around Oscar's shoulder as if to offer comfort made her feel weepy. Another symptom of hypothermia, she assumed.

Promising to return in a little while, the nurse left Kalinowski and Helene alone, closing the curtain around them.

"You've got some quick-thinking children," said Kalinowski.

"I know," replied Helene.

"And you will also need to thank your friend Alex for calling me right away."

"I have a lot to be grateful for," agreed the journalist. "But how did you find me in time?"

"You got lucky there. We were already tracking the Coast Guard vessel."

"Jeff's?"

"That's the one. We were investigating his handling of the drug smuggling cases. We suspected he was up to something — he was spending too much time near the American coast. That's why I was at the press conference the other day. He was playing the hero, but something was not quite right."

"He certainly looked like a hero."

"Never trust the handsome ones." Detective Kalinowski's words echoed the sentiment Hana had shared on the boat. Just because the archivist was a murderer didn't mean she was wrong about everything.

"When Alex called to say she thought you were in trouble and that you had gone to the breakwater, we alerted our officers in the area. And they didn't get there a moment too soon."

"I will have to thank Lee for fishing me out of the water."

"Lee? Who's Lee?" asked Kalinowski, visibly confused.

"The Coast Guard officer who saved me."

"But I've been told that you pulled yourself into the rescue boat. Kind of dived up out of the water. Like a leaping orca. A thin one, obviously. And I don't know anyone named Lee connected to this investigation."

"But at the breakwater, when I first discovered Lucy Marino's body . . . he was there. On the boat." Helene was growing more perplexed by the moment. How could Kalinowski not remember Lee?

"The only Coast Guard officer on the scene was Jeff Anders. I told you, I had to interview him afterwards because he was the first to arrive after the emergency call. Now it appears he did have a connection to Marino. That one's on me."

Helene was now beginning to seriously wonder if one of the side effects of hypothermia was having conversations that didn't make any sense. She had seen Lee. And talked with him several times. Even walked along the breakwater with him.

"Are you going to explain exactly what happened last night? We found the purse of the archivist onboard, but we think she must have ended up in the water. We haven't managed to locate her body. Or Jeff's. I presume he was there too."

Wishing she could ignore the instant replay of the Coast Guard officer being shot and then pushed over the side of the boat, Helene knew she wouldn't be able to rest properly until she had described the events to Kalinowski. She also believed that retelling a story was an important way to process trauma. Placing the words in an archive so she didn't have to bear the constant weight of carrying them around, toxic memories in a stone suitcase of grief.

As she spoke, the police officer only asked a few questions for clarity. Mostly she just scribbled furiously on the pages of her spiral notebook. The journalist came close to breaking down just once, when recalling the urgent phone call to her daughter and what it was like to hear the voice of a loved one when she was alone with a murderer.

Helene had just finished her recounting of the previous evening when the curtains around her bed were thrown open once more. Alex rushed forward to give Helene an awkward embrace, trying to avoid the IV line going into her arm. The journalist realized they were now friends who hugged. She guessed that's what happened when you both had recently come close to dying.

Beaming with a mischievous smile, Alex retrieved a package wrapped in shiny paper out of her oversized purse and handed it to Helene. "I brought you chocolates. Just seemed right for the occasion. No nuts or dairy. Or foxglove! I checked."

Detective Kalinowski raised her eyebrows. "Wow, I thought cops had a dark sense of humour. But you two are better than amateur hour in the holding cells."

"As it turns out, we are also quite good at solving crimes. Although next time wear a wetsuit, please, Helene."

Alex's comment brought back the memory of finding the life jacket in the dumpster full of Lucy Marino's discarded possessions. It made sense the curator would have one if she was spending time on boats, smuggling paintings.

"I have everything I need for now. I'll check in on you later, Helene, to see how you are doing." Kalinowski got up from the chair and tucked her notebook into one of the many pockets of her vest.

"You can feel free to check in on me later as well. To see how I am doing." Helene had witnessed a lot of shocking events in the past twenty-four hours, but watching her friend Alex openly flirt with the police officer was probably the strangest. She guessed her friend's own near-death experience had left her longing for more than hugs from friends or even cuddles from kittens.

Kalinowski cleared her throat nervously and mumbled, "Yes, there might still be some details I need to clear up with you." And then the beautiful detective fled down the hall as if she was responding to a 911 call only she could hear.

Trying to regain her friend's attention, Helene touched Alex's arm before speaking. "Thank you."

"For what?"

"For helping my kids get help."

"No problem. I'm glad it's me they called. Means a lot that I am the one they thought of. I'm not sure I've ever been someone's emergency contact before. Feels pretty good."

The Scottish nurse returned a few minutes later, shepherding along Oscar and Cleo. The medical professional stated that the doctor had given permission for

Helene to be discharged but had prescribed spending the rest of the day in bed under warm blankets. And no more swimming in the ocean until the sun came out in July.

As it turned out, Helene had her own personal heating pad in the form of her son, who nuzzled up to her in bed after arriving home. Her teenage daughter submitted to a short hug, but then played the role of a doting waiter, coming into her bedroom every fifteen minutes to offer more peppermint tea and freshly baked pumpkin muffins.

An atheist for most of her adult life, Helene gave thanks to every god she could think of, from Christian to pagan, that she had been safely returned to her home and children.

Helene was starting to doze again while Oscar watched a show on his iPad at low volume when a sudden thought brought her fully awake.

"Oscar, you remember Lee, right? The man we met on the breakwater when we went for a walk?" Hours later, Helene remained very confused as to why Detective Kalinowski did not recall the Coast Guard officer.

"The man who knew about sunsets?" asked Oscar.

"That's the one. You talked to him for a little while. I was beginning to think I was going crazy. That he didn't exist."

Oscar spoke the next words in a matter-of-fact tone that belied the profound wisdom of children. "He was there, Mom, but he also wasn't. Like when Grandma visits me sometimes but says it's our secret."

Helene was incapable of replying. Her mother had died more than three years ago. Her body was wracked by an intense shiver despite the warmth of the room and the blankets.

And then staying awake seemed too much like work, and Helene fell into a slumber deeper than any ocean.

Epilogue

It had only taken a couple days before Helene felt well enough to return to the newsroom. She was eager to write up the news story about the forgery and smuggling schemes of Lucy Marino as well as sharing the identity of the woman responsible for her death. The journalist's coverage was not going to include Marino's sabotage of the life of Benjamin Cornish. He had already suffered enough.

She was grateful when Detective Kalinowski offered to hold off sending out a police press release until the journalist had published her version of the events. It seemed a fair exchange for the role Helene had played in solving the crimes.

During their last conversation, the detective had informed Helene that the body of the archivist had not yet been recovered. Maybe it was better that Hana did not survive to witness the scandal swirling around the museum and their staff and the paintings themselves. Efforts were now being made to track down the genuine works of Amelia Grayson. Thankfully, Jeff's Coast Guard office had contained his tidy notes on everyone who had bought a smuggled painting. The missing archivist would have approved of his record keeping. Helene did have some regret that the legacy of Amelia Grayson would now be linked to these crimes.

The journalist knew she needed to write a lengthy email to Sybil Bancroft before her story went up on the internet. Nobody liked to read headlines connected to their family, even if they were long dead, without warning. Helene also felt she owed Paola Marino a conversation in case the police hadn't yet told her about Lucy being a smuggler, a forger and a blackmailer. She wondered if it might bring the woman some relief from her complicated grief to know she wasn't the only one who thought badly of her sister.

Helene was giving her article a last read before sending it off to the national editor when she decided to click on a photo Jean-Pierre had taken of Grayson's oceanscape. She enlarged the picture to fill her entire computer screen, as though the truth of its authenticity could be revealed in the brush strokes. The journalist then decided to zoom in on the figure occupying the beach, a wool hat on his head, a rope net in one hand. But when she leaned in to take a better look at the face, her heartbeat quickened. There was no mistaking the teasing smile and the sad eyes. It was Lee. In the painting. He was the fisherman.

But Lee was a ghost.

And Grayson had depicted her own fisherman.

Did this make the painting authentic or fake?

Then the two mysteries she had been carrying around in her head for the past month finally collided. Lee was short for Charlie, the companion of Amelia Grayson who had returned to protect Helene. A fisherman who had offered an artist his love and a journalist his friendship.

Helene hoped to meet him on the breakwater again one day, perhaps to share another sunset in its pink and purple ephemeral glory — a painting to be enjoyed but never possessed, its beauty immune to forgery.

If you enjoyed Blood on the Breakwater,
please leave a review on
Amazon or Goodreads.
Independent authors depend heavily
on these reviews for their success.

With gratitude,
Jean Paetkau

Kids books by Jean Paetkau:

Rumpa and the Snufflewort
The Bumwuzzle Rescue
The Snufflewort Haunting

9 781738 042200